McGinty and the Bottle Babies
By P.A. Farrell

I0543266

McGinty and the Bottle Babies

P. A. Farrell

Published by Dr. Patricia A. Farrell, 2026.

MCGINTY AND THE BOTTLE BABIES

First edition. January 30, 2026.

Copyright © 2026 P. A. Farrell.

ISBN: 979-8993739656

Written by P. A. Farrell.

Table of Contents

Chapter 1: The Day Everything Changed

The black dress itched. McGinty stood between her mother and oldest
   sister, trying not to scratch at the lace collar that pressed against
   her throat like small fingers. Three weeks had passed since the
funeral,
   but she could still smell the flowers. Lilies. They'd been everywhere,
   white and waxy, their scent so thick it had made her stomach turn.
   Her father's casket had been closed. That's what everyone kept
saying,
   as if it mattered. As if she'd wanted to see him like that, cold and
   still and not-him anymore. She"d already seen enough of not-him
in the
   months before, when the bottle had taken more and more of the
person he
   used to be.
   McGinty pressed her hand against the worn wood of the back
porch
   railing. The alley stretched out before her, a ribbon of crushed
cinders
   and shadows between the buildings. She wasn't supposed to be out
here
   alone. Not anymore. Not since.
   But the house felt too small, too full of her mother's quiet crying
and
   her sisters' careful whispers. Out here, she could breathe.
   The garage accident had happened eight months before he died.
McGinty
   remembered that day with a clarity that made her chest hurt. She'd
been
   playing jacks on the front stoop when the ambulance came, its siren
   splitting the afternoon air. Her father had been working under a car

when the jack slipped. The vehicle had come down on his leg, crushing

bone and something else, something invisible that she didn't have words

for.

After that, everything changed. He couldn't do his regular mechanic

work anymore. The leg healed crooked, and he walked with a hitch that

made him wince on cold days. More than that, though, something in his

eyes had shifted. He'd started looking past people instead of at them.

That's when Lefty from The Derby had come around. McGinty had watched

from the kitchen window as the two men talked on the front steps, her

father nodding slowly, his shoulders slumped in a way that made him look

smaller than he was. Lefty had put a hand on her father''s shoulder, squeezed once, then walked away leaving an envelope on the porch rail.

The parking lot job had been a kindness. The mafia men who ran The Derby

took care of their own, and her father had served in Korea with Lefty's

cousin. That bond meant something to them, more than most people

understood. The job was simple: sit in the little booth at the entrance

to the lot behind the stores, take money from customers, hand out

tickets. Nothing that required standing for long periods or crawling under cars.

Her father had been grateful. She'd seen it in the way he"d straightened his spine when he'd told her mother about it, in the careful way he"d dressed for his first day, putting on his cleanest shirt and the tie he"d worn to his brother"s wedding.

But the bottles had started showing up anyway. First one tucked in his lunch pail, then another in the bathroom cabinet, then more hidden in places he thought no one would look. McGinty had found them everywhere.

Under the back porch steps. Behind the loose board in the basement.

Wrapped in a towel in the garage.

She"d never told anyone about finding them. Something had stopped her each time, some sense that telling would make it more real, more permanent. As if her silence could somehow keep the truth from settling in.

The drinking had gotten worse after dark. Her father would come home from the parking lot, his breath already sweet with whiskey, and he"d head straight for the kitchen cabinet where he kept the tall bottle he didn"t bother hiding anymore. Her mother would watch him with eyes that had gone flat and distant, her mouth pressed into a thin line that never quite opened to say the words that hung between them.

McGinty had learned to read the bottles. Clear meant vodka, brown meant

whiskey, and the flat green ones meant he"d been to the package store

on the Avenue where they sold the cheap stuff that made him mean. Not

hitting-mean, not like some of the fathers she'd heard about. Just

absent-mean, the kind where he'd look right through her when she asked

him questions, as if she were made of glass.

People had started whispering. She'd caught it at school, the way

conversations would stop when she walked past, the sideways glances from

mothers picking up their children. Mrs. Sullivan from down the block had

pulled her own daughter away when McGinty had asked if she wanted to

play jump rope. The daughter had looked back over her shoulder,

confused, but Mrs. Sullivan's hand had been firm on her back, steering

her away.

McGinty hadn't understood then. She'd thought maybe she'd done

something wrong, said something she shouldn't have. It wasn't until

later, until she"d heard her mother on the phone with Aunt Rose, that

she"d understood. They were whispering about her father. About the

drinking. About how he"d been seen stumbling out of The Derby at noon,

how he"d missed two days of work at the parking lot, how Lefty had to go fetch him from the alley where he"d passed out against a dumpster.

The shame of it had burned in McGinty"s throat, hot and bitter. But

underneath the shame was something else, something that felt like loyalty mixed with anger. He was still her father. He still smiled at her sometimes, in the mornings before the first drink, when his eyes

were clear and he"d ruffle her hair and call her his McGinty-girl, the

nickname he"d given her when she was three and had insisted on wearing

his old work shirt like a dress.

The end had come quietly. No dramatic scene, no ambulance sirens this

time. He"d simply gone to sleep one night and hadn"t woken up. The

doctor had used words like liver failure and complications and years of

abuse, but McGinty had understood only one thing: he was gone.

At the funeral, Lefty had come. So had the other men from The Derby, all

of them in dark suits that looked uncomfortable on their broad frames.

They"d stood in the back of the funeral home, hats in hands, and when

it was over, Lefty had pressed an envelope into her mother"s hand. Her

mother had tried to refuse, but Lefty had closed her fingers around it

gently, his voice low and firm.

They take care of their own. That"s what her father had always said about the men from The Derby. Even now, even in death, they were keeping

that promise.

McGinty shook herself from the memory and focused on the alley below.

The sun was starting to set, painting the cinder path in shades of gold

and rust. Movement caught her eye near the back entrance to the bicycle

shop. Cardboard boxes were shifting, and she could see a figure emerging, unfolding itself from the makeshift shelter.

The Bottle Babies. That"s what everyone called them, though never to

their faces. Homeless men who lived in the alley, who slept in the recessed doorways behind the stores, who spent their days scrounging for

bottles to return for the deposit money and their nights drinking away

whatever they"d earned.

Her father had warned her about them. Stay away from those men, McGinty-girl. They"re not safe. But she"d also seen him, more than once, slip one of them a cigarette or a dollar bill. She"d watched him

stand in the alley, smoking and talking with a huge man called Rube,

their voices low and easy like old friends.

Because that"s what they"d been, she realized now with a clarity that

made her stomach drop. Her father had known them. Had maybe even been

like them, once. Before the parking lot job, before Lefty"s

intervention, before the family and the responsibilities that had kept

him tethered to something resembling normal life.

The truth of it sat heavy in her chest. Her father had been one bad day

away from sleeping in those cardboard boxes, from brewing cheap liquor

in fruit juice cans, from having people cross the street to avoid him.

McGinty descended the back porch steps slowly, her oxford shoes

crunching on the cinders as she reached the alley. She wasn"t supposed

to be out here. Her mother had been clear about that. But something

pulled her forward, some need to understand the line between her father

and these men, to see where one ended and the other began.

The figure from the cardboard boxes had fully emerged now. It was Mossy,

the one her father had warned her about most strongly. He was enormous,

not tall like Rube but wide, with a barrel chest and legs wrapped in

dirty rags. Even from a distance, she could see the dark stains on the

cloth, could smell something sour and rotten on the breeze.

Mossy turned and saw her. For a moment, they simply looked at each other

across the expanse of cinders. McGinty"s heart hammered in her chest,

every instinct screaming at her to run back to the house, to the safety

of her mother"s kitchen and her sisters" chatter.

But Mossy didn"t move toward her. He didn"t yell or curse or spit the

way she"d seen him do with other people. Instead, he lifted one gnarled

hand in a gesture that might have been a wave, might have been a warning

to stay back. Then he turned away, settling himself on an overturned

crate, his attention moving to the small fire he was coaxing to life in a rusted can.

McGinty let out a breath she hadn"t known she was holding. The fear

that had gripped her loosened slightly, replaced by something else. Curiosity, maybe. Or the beginning of understanding.

Another figure appeared from the shadows near the fish store. This one

was tall and broad, moving with a careful grace that seemed at odds with

his size. Rube. She recognized him from the times he"d talked with her

father, from the way he held himself with a dignity that his circumstances couldn"t quite erase.

Rube saw her too, and unlike Mossy, he smiled. It was a gentle smile,

the kind her father used to give her before the drinking got bad. He lifted his hand in a proper wave, and without thinking, McGinty waved

back.

The back door of the house opened behind her, and her mother"s voice

cut through the evening air, sharp with worry and anger.

McGinty! Get in this house right now!

McGinty turned and ran back up the steps, her heart pounding for a

different reason now. But as she reached the door and her mother pulled

her inside, she looked back one more time.

Rube was still standing there, watching her with an expression she couldn"t quite read. Behind him, Mossy tended his fire, and beyond them

both, the alley stretched into darkness, full of cardboard kingdoms and

broken men and stories she didn"t yet know.

Her mother closed the door firmly, turning the lock with a decisive click. But McGinty pressed her face to the window, watching until the

figures in the alley faded into shadow.

Something had shifted in her that evening, some understanding that went

deeper than words. Her father had stood in that same alley, had talked

with those same men, had shared cigarettes and stories and probably

bottles too. He"d been one of them, or close enough that it didn"t matter.

And if her father could be one of them, if a man who"d served his country and held down a job and loved his daughter could end up with a

bottle in his hand and death in his liver, then maybe those men in the

alley were more than what people said they were. Maybe they"d been

somebody"s father too, once. Maybe they"d had jobs and families and lives that had slipped away one drink at a time.

Your father was a good man. That"s what people had said at the funeral,

over and over, as if repetition could make it true, could erase the

bottles and the absences and the slow dissolution of the person he"d

been.

But watching Rube in the alley, seeing the way he"d smiled at her with

kindness in his eyes, McGinty wondered if maybe good and bad weren"t as

separate as people wanted them to be. Maybe they lived side by side in

the same person, tangled up together like the weeds that grew between

the cracks in the cinder path.

Her mother"s hand on her shoulder made her jump.

I don"t want you going near those men, her mother said quietly. Do you

understand me, McGinty?

McGinty nodded, but she didn"t turn away from the window. Her mother

sighed, a sound heavy with exhaustion and grief and worries that had no

easy solutions.

They"re not all bad, her mother said finally, her voice so soft McGinty

almost missed it. Some of them are just lost. Like your father was lost.

The words hung in the air between them, heavy with meaning. McGinty felt

her mother"s hand tighten on her shoulder, then release. Footsteps retreated into the house, leaving her alone at the window.

Outside, the alley had gone fully dark. But McGinty could still see the

faint glow of Mossy"s fire, a small point of light in the blackness.

She wondered what he was cooking in that rusted can, wondered if he"d

share it with Rube, wondered if they talked about their lives before or

if the past was something they"d learned to leave behind with their former names and addresses.

Her father had never talked about his past much. She knew he"d grown up

poor, that he"d served in Korea, that he"d learned to fix cars in the Army. But there were gaps in the story, years that he"d never mentioned, times he"d skipped over in conversation. She wondered now if

those gaps had been filled with bottles and alleys and cardboard boxes,

if he"d climbed out once only to slip back toward the edge.

The parking lot job had been a lifeline. She understood that now. Lefty

and the men from The Derby had thrown him a rope when he was drowning,

had pulled him back to shore and given him a reason to stay there. It

had worked for a while. Almost long enough.

McGinty pressed her hand against the cold glass of the window. Three

weeks since the funeral. Three weeks of watching her mother count pennies at the kitchen table, of wearing her sisters" hand-me-downs instead of the new shoes she"d been promised, of understanding in new and terrible ways that her father"s death had left them in a precarious

place.

But Lefty"s envelope had helped. So had the food that appeared on their

doorstep from neighbors, the fish store owner who"d knocked off half

their bill, the landlord who"d told her mother not to worry about next

month"s rent. The web of kindness that caught them wasn"t official or

organized. It was simply people taking care of people, the same way her

father had once taken care of Rube and the others, sharing cigarettes in

the alley when he had them, passing along day-old bread from the bakery

where he"d once worked.

The cycle kept turning, McGinty thought. Help given and received,

dignity preserved in small gestures, survival dependent on the kindness

of people who barely had enough for themselves.

She pulled away from the window finally, her breath leaving a faint fog

on the glass. Tomorrow she"d go to school and pretend not to notice

when conversations stopped as she approached. She"d play by herself at

recess and do her homework at the kitchen table while her mother sorted

through bills. She"d be good, be quiet, be no trouble to anyone.

But in her heart, something had changed. She"d stood in the alley and

looked at the Bottle Babies, and instead of seeing monsters or threats,

she"d seen men. Broken men, lost men, men who were fighting to survive

in the only ways they knew how.

Men like her father had been. Men he might have become entirely, if not

for Lefty and the parking lot and the thin thread of luck that had kept

him from sliding all the way down.

McGinty climbed the stairs to the bedroom she shared with her sisters,

each step creaking under her weight. The black funeral dress lay across

her chair, waiting to be hung up. She touched it briefly, remembering

the scratch of lace, the smell of lilies, the weight of goodbye.

Everything had changed the day her father died. But maybe, she thought

as she changed into her nightgown and slipped under the thin covers,

maybe some things had changed before that. Maybe they"d been changing

all along, and she"d only just now learned to see them.

In the alley below, Mossy"s fire continued to burn, a small defiant

light against the darkness. And somewhere in the shadows, Rube settled

into his cardboard kingdom, preparing for another night of survival.

They were still there. They would be there tomorrow. And McGinty, lying

in her bed with her sisters breathing softly beside her, knew she would

see them again.

Chapter 2: The Alley Kingdom

The alley ran the length of the block, a narrow corridor between her
world and the Avenue where proper people shopped and walked
and
pretended not to see the shadows. McGinty stood at her back gate,
her
hand on the peeling paint of the latch, and studied the geography
of her
kingdom.
Because that"s what it was, really. Her kingdom. The place she
knew
better than anyone else in her family, better even than her sisters
who
were old enough to venture onto the Avenue alone. They saw the
alley as
something to avoid, a necessary path to the garbage cans and
nothing
more. But McGinty saw the truth of it, the hidden world that
existed in
plain sight.
The cinders crunched underfoot, a mix of coal ash and gravel that
the
city had laid down years ago and never bothered to replace. In dry
weather, the path turned to dust that coated everything in a fine
gray
powder. In rain, it became a treacherous mud slick that would ruin
her
oxford shoes if she wasn"t careful. She"d learned to read the
cinders,
to know where the firm patches were and where the loose ash
would give

way beneath her weight.

To her left, the back of her own house rose up, weathered clapboard that

her mother kept as clean as poverty would allow. The porch sagged

slightly in the middle, and the stairs creaked on the second and fourth

step. McGinty knew which boards were solid and which ones would betray

her presence with their groans.

Beyond their house stretched the parking lot, a vast expanse of cracked

asphalt where her father had spent his days in the small booth at the

entrance. She couldn''t see the booth from here, but she knew it was

there, empty now. Someone else would take the job eventually. Lefty

would find another veteran who needed the work, another man with a story

written in scars and silences.

To her right, the alley continued toward the Avenue, lined with the back

entrances to stores. The bicycle shop came first, its loading dock

elevated three feet off the ground. Cardboard boxes were stacked against

the wall, the ones that bikes came in, long and wide and perfect for

sleeping. That''s where Mossy lived, in the depression of the stairwell

that led down to the shop''s back door.

Next came the toy store, then the fish market with its perpetual smell of brine and old ice. The Chinese restaurant was above the fish market,

accessible only by the black metal fire escape that zigzagged up the side of the building. McGinty had climbed those stairs more times than

she could count, fetching chicken chow mein in a metal pail, her heart

racing with fear of the darkness and the unknown.

At the far end, where the alley opened onto the Avenue, sat The Derby.

From the outside, it looked like any other storefront, with its painted

window and modest sign. But McGinty knew better. Everyone knew better.

The Derby was where the bookies worked, where men placed bets on horses

and baseball games, where money changed hands under the table and the

law looked the other way because everyone was getting their cut.

Her father had told her stories about The Derby, back before the accident, back when he"d still talked to her about things. He"d

explained how it worked, how men like Lefty and Tony and Big Pete ran an

operation that was technically illegal but somehow also necessary. They

kept the neighborhood safe, he"d said. They made sure other criminals

stayed away, made sure the store owners didn"t get shaken down by outside gangs, made sure people like him had jobs when regular work

dried up.

It was complicated, he"d said. Like most things that mattered, it existed in shades of gray rather than the black and white that teachers

talked about at school.

McGinty took a step into the alley, then another. The morning sun cast

long shadows from the buildings, creating patterns of light and dark

across the cinder path. She moved slowly, letting her eyes adjust,

watching for movement in the doorways and behind the dumpsters.

There. Near the bicycle shop, a figure was stirring. Not Mossy, she

thought. This person was too tall, too careful in their movements. She

moved closer, staying near the wall of her own building, ready to bolt

back to the house if needed.

It was Rube. She recognized his size first, the broad shoulders and

massive frame that made him look like he should be working construction

instead of sleeping in an alley. He was washing his face at a spigot
that jutted from the back of the fish market, the cold water running
over his hands as he splashed it onto his cheeks and neck.

The sight surprised her. She"d expected the Bottle Babies to be dirty,

disheveled, to smell as bad up close as they sometimes did from a

distance. But Rube was methodical about his washing, using a scrap of

cloth that might have once been a shirt to scrub at his arms and face.

His hair, while long, was combed back from his forehead. His clothes,

though worn and patched, were relatively clean.

He looked up and saw her watching. For a moment, neither of them moved.

Then Rube smiled, the same gentle smile from the night before, and

lifted his hand in greeting.

Morning, Little Miss, he called softly.

Little Miss. That"s what he"d called her father"s daughter. That"s what she was to him.

Morning, she replied, her voice smaller than she"d intended.

Rube turned off the spigot and wrung out his cloth. He seemed to be

debating something, his large hands working the fabric as he thought.

Finally, he spoke again.

I was sorry about your dad. He was a good man.

The words everyone said at funerals. But coming from Rube, they sounded

different. Real, somehow. As if he"d actually known her father, not just passed him on the street.

Did you know him? McGinty asked before she could stop herself.

Rube nodded slowly. We"d talk sometimes. He"d give me a cigarette when

he had one. Tell me about Korea. We were both there, you know. Different

times, but same war. He understood.

Understood what?

Rube looked away, toward the parking lot where McGinty"s father had

worked. How hard it is to come back from something like that. How the

world keeps moving but you get stuck somewhere, and you can"t quite catch up no matter how hard you try.

The honesty of it took McGinty"s breath away. This was more than her

father had ever told her about the war, more than anyone had been willing to say. It was as if Rube, having nothing left to lose, could afford to tell the truth.

Movement behind Rube caught her attention. Another figure was emerging

from a different doorway, this one shorter and thinner, with a pronounced limp. The Butcher. McGinty had heard the name whispered with

a mix of fear and distaste, though she"d never understood why he was

called that.

The Butcher hobbled forward on a single crutch, his right pant leg pinned up at the knee to show where his leg should have been. He moved

with a practiced efficiency, swinging his body forward and planting the

crutch, then bringing his good leg around. As he got closer, McGinty

could see that his face was weathered and lined, but his eyes were sharp

and calculating.

Morning, Rube, The Butcher said, then noticed McGinty. Well, well. The

little McGinty girl. You staying out of trouble?

His voice wasn"t unfriendly, but it wasn"t warm either. McGinty nodded, not trusting herself to speak. She"d been warned about The

Butcher specifically, told that he had a temper and wasn"t to be trusted.

But as she watched him lean against the wall of the fish market, pulling

out a bent cigarette and straightening it carefully before lighting it, she saw only a tired man trying to make it through another day. The morning sun caught the metal of his crutch, and she noticed it was worn

smooth where his hand gripped it, the rubber pad at the bottom nearly

gone from use.

You got a smoke for me? The Butcher asked Rube.

Rube shook his head. Fresh out. Fish store might give you one if you

sweep their front step.

The Butcher grunted, neither agreeing nor disagreeing. He took a long

drag on his own cigarette, savoring it, making it last. McGinty watched

the smoke curl up toward the sky, dissipating in the morning air.

A third figure shuffled into view, this one smaller and frailer than the

others. Jimmy. McGinty knew him by sight and by story. He"d been a

friend of someone in her mother"s family, years ago, before the

drinking took him down. Now he lived in the alley like the rest, though

he seemed to have one foot still in the world of regular people, doing

odd jobs at The Derby and sleeping in slightly better spots than Mossy

or The Butcher.

Jimmy"s hands trembled as he approached, his whole body seeming to vibrate with some internal frequency that wouldn"t quiet. His eyes darted from Rube to The Butcher to McGinty, never quite settling on any

of them for long.

Morning, he mumbled, his voice so soft McGinty almost missed it.

The men responded with nods and grunts, a communication that needed no

words. They"d lived together in this alley long enough to develop their

own language, their own understanding of boundaries and courtesies.

McGinty stood watching them, these men her mother had warned her about,

these Bottle Babies who were supposed to be dangerous and unpredictable.

But all she saw were three tired people trying to find their footing for

another day, no different really from her mother counting pennies at the

kitchen table or her sisters sharing a single pair of good shoes between

them.

A door slammed somewhere, and all four of them turned toward the sound.

Mossy was emerging from his cardboard fortress, unwinding himself from

the boxes with the slow deliberation of someone in pain. Even from this

distance, McGinty could see the rags wrapped around his legs, could

smell the sour-sweet scent of infection carried on the breeze.

The other men tensed immediately. Rube straightened to his full height.

The Butcher gripped his crutch a little tighter. Jimmy took a small step

backward, his trembling increasing.

Mossy surveyed his domain with eyes that were both shrewd and clouded.

He spotted McGinty and the others, and for a moment his face twisted

into something that might have been anger or might have been pain. It

was hard to tell with Mossy. Everything about him was hard to read, as

if years of drinking had blurred the lines between his emotions until

they all looked the same.

But then his gaze moved past them, dismissing them as not worth his

immediate attention. He had more pressing matters to attend to, namely

the small fire he was building in his rusted can and the mysterious brew

he was starting to cook.

McGinty, her mother"s voice cut through the morning air, sharp and

worried. What are you doing out there?

McGinty turned to see her mother standing on the back porch, arms

crossed over her chest. She looked small from this distance, smaller

than McGinty remembered, as if the weeks since her father"s death had

somehow shrunk her.

Just looking, McGinty called back.

Well, stop looking and get in here. You need to get ready for school.

McGinty glanced back at Rube and the others. They"d already turned

away, going about their morning routines as if she"d never been there.

Only Rube looked back, lifting his hand in a small wave before moving

toward the fish market, probably to see about that sweeping job in exchange for a cigarette.

She trudged back to the house, her shoes kicking up small clouds of cinder dust. Her mother waited at the door, holding it open with an

expression that mixed relief and exasperation.

I don"t want you talking to those men, her mother said as McGinty climbed the steps.

Rube knew Dad, McGinty said.

Her mother"s face tightened, and for a moment McGinty thought she might

get angry. But instead, her mother just sighed and pulled her into the

house.

I know he did, her mother said softly. Your father talked to all of

them. He used to be one of them, before we met. Before he had you girls

to come home to.

The admission hung in the air between them. McGinty had suspected as

much, but hearing it confirmed was different. It made it real in a way

her suspicions never had.

He lived in the alley? McGinty asked.

For a while, yes. After Korea, before he got steady work. He"d sleep in

doorways and drink whatever he could afford. Then he met me, and he

tried to be better. He was better, for a long time.

Until the accident.

Her mother nodded, not trusting herself to speak. She turned away, busying herself with breakfast preparations, but McGinty could see the

way her shoulders shook slightly, the way her hands trembled as she reached for the bread box.

McGinty wanted to hug her mother, wanted to say something comforting,

but she didn"t know what words would help. So she went upstairs to

change for school, leaving her mother alone in the kitchen with her grief and her memories.

As she pulled on her school dress and buckled her oxford shoes, McGinty

thought about what her mother had said. Her father had been one of them.

He"d slept in cardboard boxes and drunk cheap wine and lived day to day

with no thought for the future. And then something had changed. He"d

met her mother, and that had been enough reason to try.

For a while, it had been enough. He"d held down jobs, paid rent, raised

three daughters. He"d been present, mostly. He"d been a father.

But the accident had broken something in him, some fragile thing that had been holding him together. And once broken, it couldn"t be fixed.

The drinking had come back, not all at once, but gradually, like water

seeping through a cracked dam. First a few bottles, then more, then the

inability to stop even when he wanted to.

The parking lot job had been a lifeline, but even lifelines could fray. And in the end, it hadn"t been enough to save him.

McGinty finished dressing and went back downstairs. Her mother had laid

out breakfast, such as it was. Day-old bread toasted over the stove, margarine spread thin, a glass of milk that had been watered down to

make it last longer. It wasn"t much, but it was what they had.

Her sisters joined them, and they ate in silence, each lost in their own

thoughts. The kitchen felt emptier without their father at the head of

the table, even though he hadn"t really been present for meals in months before he died. His absence was a physical thing, a hole in the

fabric of their morning routine.

After breakfast, McGinty gathered her school things and prepared to face

another day of whispers and sideways glances. But before she left, she

paused at the back window, looking out at the alley one more time.

The Bottle Babies were still there, going about their business. Rube was

sweeping the front of the fish market, his broad back bent to the task.

The Butcher had hobbled off somewhere, probably to panhandle on the

Avenue. Jimmy was sitting on an overturned crate, his hands still

trembling, staring at nothing. And Mossy was tending his fire, adding

something to his rusted can that steamed and smoked in the morning air.

They were her neighbors, McGinty realized. Not in the traditional sense,

perhaps. They didn"t live in houses with addresses and mailboxes. But

they lived here, in this alley that was as much a part of her world as the kitchen she stood in or the school she was about to walk to.

And if her father had been one of them once, if the line between her

family and those men was as thin as a parking lot job and a few years of

sobriety, then maybe they deserved more than fear and avoidance. Maybe

they deserved to be seen as people, complicated and flawed and struggling, but people nonetheless.

McGinty, her mother called. You"re going to be late.

McGinty turned away from the window and headed for the front door. But

the image of the alley stayed with her, the geography of her kingdom

mapped in her mind with new clarity and understanding.

It was more than just a path between buildings. It was a world unto itself, with its own residents and rules and quiet dignities. And she was part of it, whether she wanted to be or not.

Chapter 3: Mossy"s Domain

McGinty clutched the metal beer pail against her chest, feeling its
weight and the cold seeping through her thin sweater. Inside,
chicken
chow mein sloshed gently with each careful step she took. A
dollar"s
worth of dinner for the whole family. The paper bag with the rice
and
fortune cookies crinkled in her other hand.

She stood at the bottom of the fire escape, two stories up from
Mossy"s
domain, trying to work up the courage to descend. The black metal
stairs
gleamed dully in the fading daylight, and below, she could see the
familiar pile of cardboard boxes that marked Mossy"s territory.

He was there. She could see movement, could smell the distinctive
odor
that announced his presence like a warning sign. Rotting flesh
mixed
with old alcohol and unwashed clothes. The smell traveled up the
fire
escape and made her eyes water.

McGinty took a deep breath through her mouth and started down.
Each step
rang out against the metal, announcing her approach. There was no
way to
be quiet on this staircase. No way to slip past unnoticed.

As she descended, she thought about what she knew of Mossy. Not
much,
really. Just stories whispered by her mother and overheard in

conversations between adults who thought children weren"t listening.

He"d been in World War I, they said. Had come back different, the way

men did from wars. Had started drinking to forget whatever he"d seen

over there in the trenches, and the drinking had never stopped.

His real name was Morris, or maybe Morton. No one seemed to remember

anymore. He"d been Mossy for so long that his given name had faded away

like everything else about his former life.

The legs were the worst part. McGinty had seen them from a distance, but

up close they were horrifying. Purple and red sores covered his calves,

weeping a yellowish fluid that soaked through the dirty rags he used as

bandages. The infection had a smell all its own, sweet and rotten like

fruit left too long in the sun.

Diabetes, she"d heard her mother say to Aunt Rose on the phone. And he

won"t get it treated. Just drinks more and lets it get worse.

McGinty reached the halfway point on the stairs. From here, she had a

clear view of Mossy"s setup. The cardboard boxes were arranged with

surprising care, tucked into the depression of the stairwell that led

down to the bicycle shop"s back door. The boxes were the large ones that bikes came in, six feet long and three feet high, perfect for a man

to curl up inside.

He had a system, she realized. The boxes weren"t just thrown together

randomly. He"d created a shelter, using the cement walls of the
stairwell as windbreaks and the boxes as a roof. It was crude but
effective, protecting him from rain and snow and the worst of the cold.

His cooking area was set up a few feet away from his sleeping spot. The

rusted can sat on a makeshift platform of bricks, with a small fire
burning underneath. Fruit juice cans lined the wall behind him, his
precious stock of Sneaky Pete stored away from prying eyes.

Mossy looked up as she passed, his eyes tracking her movement. For a

heart-stopping moment, McGinty thought he might say something, might

reach out and grab her. She froze on the stairs, the beer pail suddenly

feeling very heavy in her arms.

But Mossy just watched her with those clouded eyes, his face unreadable.

Then he turned back to his fire, dismissing her as not worth his
attention.

McGinty let out a breath she hadn"t known she was holding and continued

down the stairs. Her legs were shaking by the time she reached the
bottom, and she had to pause to steady herself before heading up the

alley toward home.

As she walked, she thought about what she"d just seen. The careful arrangement of the boxes. The organized cooking area. The way Mossy had

looked at her without threat, just acknowledgment. It wasn"t what she"d expected. None of this was what she"d expected.

The next day, McGinty found herself in the alley again. Not because she

had to be there, but because something drew her back. A curiosity, maybe. Or a need to understand these men who lived in her neighborhood"s shadows.

She positioned herself near her back gate, far enough from Mossy to feel

safe but close enough to observe. Rube was there, talking with The Butcher near the fish market. Jimmy was somewhere out of sight, probably

at The Derby doing whatever odd jobs they needed.

Mossy emerged from his cardboard shelter, moving with the slow deliberation of someone in constant pain. He"d removed the rags from

his legs, and McGinty could see the full extent of the damage. The sores

were worse than she"d thought, some of them deep enough that she could

see tissue beneath the skin.

How did he stand it? How did he walk around with legs like that, refusing treatment, refusing help? The pain must be constant, overwhelming. Yet here he was, tending his fire, preparing his brew, going about his day as if his body wasn"t slowly destroying itself.

The Butcher hobbled over to Mossy"s area, his crutch clicking against

the cinders. McGinty watched as the two men engaged in what looked like

a negotiation. The Butcher gesturing, Mossy shaking his head, The

Butcher pulling out a coin and holding it up.

Finally, Mossy nodded. He reached behind his boxes and pulled out one of

the fruit juice cans, smaller than the others. He poured a measure of

dark liquid into a tin cup and handed it to The Butcher, who downed it

in one gulp, his face contorting at the taste.

The Butcher handed over the coin, and Mossy tucked it away somewhere in

his layers of clothing. The transaction complete, The Butcher hobbled

off, moving with slightly more steadiness than before.

So that was Sneaky Pete. Whatever Mossy cooked in those cans, it was

strong enough to steady a man"s nerves, to chase away the shakes and

the fears and the memories that haunted them all. It was medicine and

poison rolled into one, bought with dimes and quarters and desperate

need.

McGinty watched as another customer approached, this one a stranger to

her. A younger man, not quite as weathered as the others, with clothes

that suggested he hadn"t been homeless long. He looked nervous as he

neared Mossy"s domain, his hands fidgeting at his sides.

Mossy eyed him with suspicion, his body language closing off. He said something McGinty couldn"t hear, and the young man backed away quickly,

nearly tripping over his own feet in his haste to leave.

Rube appeared then, having finished his work at the fish market. He said

something to Mossy, his tone easy and conversational. Mossy"s posture

relaxed slightly, and he nodded toward his cooking area.

Rube settled himself on an overturned crate a respectful distance away.

They didn"t speak much, these two men. But they didn"t need to.

They"d lived in this alley long enough to develop an understanding, a

way of being near each other without crowding, without demanding more

than the other could give.

McGinty realized she was watching a kind of ecosystem, a delicate

balance of power and need and mutual respect. Mossy was the center of

it, the one with the product everyone wanted. But he didn"t abuse that

power. He charged fair prices, kept his word about the quality of his

brew, and protected his territory from outsiders.

In return, the others gave him space. They didn"t steal from him,

didn"t challenge him, didn"t try to take over his spot. The Butcher

might argue over prices, but he always paid. Jimmy might be nervous

around him, but he never tried to undercut Mossy"s business. And Rube,

big enough to be a threat to anyone, treated Mossy with a courtesy that bordered on friendship.

A door opened above, and the owner of the Chinese restaurant stepped

onto the fire escape. He was carrying a bag of garbage, which he

proceeded to throw into the dumpster below. His eyes swept the alley,

taking in the usual residents, and he sighed heavily.

But he didn"t call the police. He didn"t tell them to leave. He just

went back inside, closing the door behind him with a tired resignation.

McGinty had wondered about that. Why did the store owners tolerate the

Bottle Babies? Why not call the cops and have them cleared out?

Watching Mossy in his domain, she began to understand. The bicycle shop

owner had an expensive inventory and a back door that was less secure

than the front. The toy store dealt in easily stolen merchandise. Even

the fish market, with its cash register and valuable equipment, was vulnerable.

But who would be brave enough or stupid enough to break into a store

when Mossy was sleeping right there in the doorway? Who would risk

encountering a man who smelled like death, who had nothing to lose, who

would yell and curse and wake the whole neighborhood?

The Bottle Babies were better than guard dogs. They were protection that

didn"t need to be fed or trained. They just needed to be left alone to their cardboard kingdoms and their desperate trades.

It was a symbiotic relationship, McGinty realized. The stores got protection, and the Bottle Babies got a place to sleep. Every once in a
while, a store owner would slip one of them a dollar or give them a meal. Not out of kindness exactly, but out of the understanding that you
took care of the things that protected you.

Mossy must have felt her watching because he turned and looked directly
at her. McGinty froze, caught in his gaze. His eyes were milky and unfocused, the whites yellowed from years of drinking. But there was
something in them, some spark of awareness that hadn"t been completely
drowned.

He lifted one gnarled hand, not quite a wave but an acknowledgment. She
was there, and he saw her, and that was enough. Then he turned back to
his fire, stirring whatever concoction was brewing in his can.

McGinty let out a breath. Her heart was pounding, but not entirely from
fear. There was something else there now, something that felt like the
beginning of understanding.

That evening at dinner, McGinty asked her mother about the war. About
World War I specifically, about what her grandfather had experienced
when he"d served.

Her mother set down her fork, surprised by the question. Why do
you want
to know about that?
I was just wondering, McGinty said. About Grandpa. About what
it was
like.
Her mother was quiet for a moment, considering. He didn"t talk
about it
much, she finally said. When he came home, he wasn"t the same as
when
he left. Your grandmother said it was like living with a stranger for
the first few years. He"d wake up screaming. Couldn"t stand loud
noises. Jumped at shadows.
But he got better?
He learned to live with it. Had your grandmother to help him, and
his
faith. Some men didn"t have that. Some men came back and had
nothing to
hold onto, so they drowned themselves in bottles.
Like Mossy, McGinty thought but didn"t say. Her grandfather had
been
lucky. He"d had people and purpose and enough strength to resist
the
pull of alcohol. But Mossy hadn"t. Or maybe he"d tried and failed.
Maybe he"d fought that battle and lost, and now here he was,
decades
later, still paying the price for things he"d seen in trenches half a
world away.
That night, McGinty dreamed about the alley. In her dream, Mossy
stood
at the center of his domain, but his legs were healed and his eyes
were

clear. He was cooking something over his fire, but instead of Sneaky
Pete, it was a proper stew that smelled of herbs and vegetables.

People came to him one by one. The Butcher, Jimmy, Rube. Even
her father

appeared, looking as he had before the accident, before the
drinking got

bad. They all sat around the fire, sharing the meal, talking in low
voices about things McGinty couldn"t quite hear.

When she woke, the dream faded but the feeling lingered. There
had been

something peaceful about it, something that suggested these men
had once

been different people, had once sat around fires and shared meals
in

circumstances far removed from this alley.

McGinty got up and went to the window. The sun was just rising,
painting

the alley in shades of gold and amber. She could see Mossy"s boxes,
could see the smoke from his morning fire beginning to rise.

He was still there. Still breathing, still surviving. And in that
survival was a kind of defiance, a refusal to simply lie down and die
despite the pain and the sickness and the decades of hardship.

McGinty thought about her father, about how he"d fought his own
battle

with alcohol and ultimately lost. But at least he"d had the parking
lot

job. At least he"d had Lefty and the men from The Derby looking
out for

him. At least he"d had a family to try for, even if the trying hadn"t
been enough in the end.

Mossy had none of that. Whatever family he"d once had was long
gone,

whatever friends he"d made had drifted away or died. All he had was his

cardboard kingdom and his Sneaky Pete and the other Bottle Babies who

shared his alley.

And yet he persisted. Day after day, year after year, he woke up and

tended his fire and cooked his brew and defended his small patch of

territory against all comers.

There was something almost noble about it, McGinty thought. Something

that deserved respect, even if the world refused to give it.

She watched until her mother called her for breakfast, then turned away

from the window. But the image of Mossy"s domain stayed with her, a

reminder that even in the darkest corners, even among the most broken

people, there was still a spark of something worth seeing.

Chapter 4: Rube"s Gentle Giant

Rube stood near the edge of the parking lot, his massive frame blocking
out the sun. He was six-foot-six at least, with shoulders broad
enough
that McGinty wondered how he fit through regular doorways. His
arms were
thick with muscle despite the months of irregular meals, and dark
hair
covered them from wrist to shoulder. His chin was prominent and
square,
the kind of jaw that suggested strength even when the rest of him
suggested defeat.

McGinty had been watching him for days now, trying to work up
the
courage to approach. He seemed different from the others, more
present
somehow. He washed regularly at the spigot, kept his clothes as
clean as
circumstances allowed, and never seemed to get as drunk as Mossy
or The
Butcher. There was a steadiness to Rube that the others lacked, as if
some part of him remained tethered to the world of regular people
even
while he lived in cardboard boxes.

She"d brought the baseball mitt with her, the first baseman"s glove
that had been donated to the church team. They"d given it to her
when
she"d begged, even though they"d made it clear she could never
actually play on the team. Girls didn"t play baseball. Girls cheered
from the sidelines or kept score or brought orange slices for
halftime.

But they didn"t play.

Still, the mitt was hers, and she"d been practicing with it against the

brick wall of her house when no one was watching. She could catch pretty

well now, her hand automatically positioning itself under the ball, her

fingers closing at just the right moment to secure it in the glove"s pocket.

But throwing against a wall wasn"t the same as playing catch with

another person. She needed someone to practice with, someone who

wouldn"t laugh at her or tell her she should be playing with dolls instead.

Rube seemed like he might understand. He"d been a soldier, after all.

Soldiers played ball in their downtime, didn"t they? She"d seen

pictures in magazines of servicemen throwing around a baseball between

missions, smiling despite whatever horrors they"d witnessed.

McGinty took a deep breath and walked toward him, the mitt dangling from

one hand and the baseball clutched in the other.

Rube saw her coming and straightened up from where he"d been sorting

through a box of returnable bottles. His face softened into that gentle

smile she"d seen before, the one that made her think of her father in

his better moments.

Morning, Little Miss, he said, his voice deep and warm. What brings you out here today?

McGinty held up the mitt and baseball. I was wondering if maybe you"d

want to play catch?

The question hung in the air between them. For a moment, Rube just

stared at her, and McGinty was afraid he"d say no. Afraid he"d laugh

or tell her to go bother someone else or say something mean about girls

not belonging on baseball diamonds.

But then Rube"s smile widened, and he nodded slowly. You know what?

I"d like that very much. Haven"t thrown a ball in years.

McGinty"s face lit up. She handed him the mitt, and he took it carefully, his large hands dwarfing the leather glove. He worked his fingers into it, adjusting the fit, testing the pocket with his other hand.

This is a good mitt, he said approvingly. First baseman"s glove. You planning on playing first base?

They won"t let me play at all, McGinty admitted. But I want to be ready, just in case.

Rube"s expression turned thoughtful. That"s the spirit. You practice

anyway, and one day maybe they"ll change their minds. Or maybe you"ll

find a place where girls can play too.

They positioned themselves on the edge of the parking lot, standing on

the crushed cinders that separated the asphalt from the alley. McGinty

braced herself, ready for the first throw.

Rube wound up and threw, a gentle lob that gave McGinty plenty
of time

to position herself under it. But as the ball left his hand, something
went wrong. Maybe he"d put too much force behind it out of habit.
Maybe

his aim was off after years without practice. Whatever the reason,
the

ball came in fast and high.

McGinty tried to adjust, tried to move quickly enough to get her
mitt

up. But the cinders shifted under her oxford shoes, unstable and
treacherous. Her ankle turned slightly, throwing off her balance.
Instead of landing safely in her mitt, the ball hit her squarely in the
mouth.

The impact was shocking, a burst of pain that made her eyes water.
She

tasted blood immediately, sweet and coppery, leaking into her
mouth from

where her lip had split against her teeth. The mitt fell from her
hand

as she stumbled backward, trying to process what had just
happened.

McGinty! Rube"s voice cracked with panic. He was running
toward her,

his massive feet pounding across the cinders. Oh God, Little Miss,
I

didn"t mean it! I didn"t mean to hurt you!

She looked up through watering eyes to see tears streaming down
Rube"s

face. Actual tears, cutting tracks through the dust on his cheeks.
His

huge hands were raised as if he wanted to reach for her but was afraid

to touch her, afraid he"d cause more damage with his size and strength.

The sight of this giant man crying over her stopped McGinty"s own tears

before they could really start. She"d been about to cry, about to run home and hide her injury and never come back to the alley. But seeing

Rube"s distress, seeing the genuine agony on his face, made her own pain seem less important.

I"m sorry, I"m so sorry, Rube was saying, his voice thick with emotion. I didn"t mean it. Please, please don"t cry. I"ll never forgive myself if you"re hurt bad.

McGinty wiped her mouth with her sleeve, relieved to see only a small

amount of blood on the fabric. Inside her mouth, she could feel a bump

where the ball had caught her lip against her teeth. It hurt, but not terribly. She"d had worse injuries from falling off her bike or tripping on the sidewalk.

It"s okay, she managed to say, though her split lip made the words come

out funny. I"m okay. It doesn"t hurt that much.

But Rube was inconsolable. He"d dropped to his knees in the cinders,

his big body folding down until he was at her eye level. The tears kept

coming, and he was twisting his hands together in a gesture of such pure

anguish that McGinty found herself reaching out to pat his shoulder.

Really, it"s fine, she insisted. It was an accident. You didn"t mean
to do it.

But I hurt you, Rube said. I hurt a little girl. What kind of man does
that?

McGinty understood then. This wasn"t just about her split lip. This
was

about something deeper, some guilt or shame that Rube carried
with him.

Maybe about his own child, the son he"d mentioned but rarely saw.
Maybe

about things he"d done in the war, people he"d hurt when he"d had
to.

Whatever the source, the pain in his eyes was real and
overwhelming.

Let"s play catch some more, McGinty said firmly. I want to keep
playing.

Rube looked at her as if she"d suggested something impossible. You
want

to keep playing? After what I just did?

It was an accident, McGinty repeated. And I want to learn. But
maybe you

could stand closer? And throw underhand?

The suggestion brought a flicker of hope to Rube"s face. He wiped
his

eyes with the back of his hand and slowly got to his feet. You"re
sure?

You really want to keep going?

McGinty nodded, picking up her mitt and positioning herself
carefully on

more stable ground. Yeah. Let"s go. You stand right there, she
pointed

to a spot only about fifteen feet away, close enough that he"d have to

throw underhand.

Rube moved to the indicated spot, and they began again. This time his

throws were gentle, controlled, lobbing the ball in a soft arc that gave

McGinty plenty of time to position herself. They fell into a rhythm, the

ball sailing back and forth between them, and gradually the tension eased.

That"s it, Rube encouraged. You"re getting the hang of it. Keep your

eye on the ball all the way into your mitt.

They played for about twenty minutes before McGinty"s arm started to

tire. The cut inside her lip throbbed with each throw, but she didn"t mention it. This felt important somehow, continuing despite the pain. It

felt like proving something, though she wasn"t entirely sure what.

Finally, Rube called it quits. You did real good, Little Miss. Got a good arm on you. Better rest it now though, don"t want to strain anything.

McGinty retrieved her mitt and ball, tucking them under her arm. Thanks

for playing with me.

Rube"s face was serious as he looked down at her. Thank you for giving

me another chance. For not being afraid of me after I hurt you. That

means more than you know.

Over the next few weeks, they established a routine. Whenever Rube had

time, whenever he wasn"t working his odd jobs at the fish market or The

Derby, he"d meet McGinty in the parking lot for a game of catch. They

never talked about much beyond the mechanics of throwing and catching,

but the silence between them was comfortable.

McGinty learned more about Rube through observation than conversation.

She noticed how he never drank during the day when he had work lined up.

How he"d save whatever money he earned, keeping it in a small pouch

tucked inside his shirt. How he"d disappear sometimes on Saturday afternoons and come back looking both happy and sad, as if he"d been

somewhere that brought him joy and pain in equal measure.

One Saturday, she saw him talking with a woman and a young boy near the

entrance to the alley. The woman looked tired and worn, her teeth stained and broken in the way that marked her as an alcoholic. But the

boy was different. He was clean and well-dressed, with carefully combed

dark hair and shoes that looked new.

The boy ran to Rube, wrapping his arms around Rube"s legs in a hug.

Rube lifted him up effortlessly, spinning him around as the boy laughed.

The sound of that laughter echoed through the alley, pure and joyful,

and McGinty saw Rube"s face transform with love.

That was his son. That"s who Rube was working for, who he was staying

sober for during the day. That"s why he saved his money and kept

himself as clean and presentable as circumstances allowed. He was trying

to be a father despite living in a cardboard box.

McGinty watched as Rube pulled out his money pouch and counted bills

into the woman"s hand. The woman said something, and Rube shook his

head firmly. More bills appeared, until the woman nodded and tucked the

money away. She said something else, gesturing to the boy, and Rube

knelt down to speak with his son directly.

The conversation lasted only a few minutes, then the woman was pulling

the boy away. The boy looked back over his shoulder, waving, and Rube

waved back until they"d disappeared around the corner.

Rube stood there for a long moment after they"d gone, his massive

shoulders slumped. Then he turned and saw McGinty watching. For a

second, something like shame crossed his face. But McGinty smiled at

him, a genuine smile of understanding, and Rube"s expression softened.

That"s my boy, he said simply. My son. I don"t get to see him much, but I try to give his mother money when I can. For shoes and things he

needs.

He looked like a nice boy, McGinty offered.

He is. He"s a good kid. Deserves better than what I can give him. But I

try. Lord knows I try.

The parallel to her own father hit McGinty with unexpected force. Her

father had tried too. He"d held down the parking lot job, brought home

a paycheck, put food on the table. He"d tried to be present, to be sober, to be the man his family needed.

But trying hadn"t been enough. The accident had broken something in

him, and the drinking had filled the cracks. In the end, he"d failed despite his best efforts, and his family had been left to pick up the pieces.

Rube was failing too, in a way. He was homeless, alcoholic, living day

to day with no real prospects for improvement. But he was also still trying. Still working odd jobs, still saving money for his son, still showing up for those brief Saturday visits.

Maybe that"s what mattered, McGinty thought. Not whether you succeeded

or failed, but whether you kept trying. Whether you showed up, even when

showing up meant facing your own inadequacy and shame.

Want to throw a few? Rube asked, pulling McGinty from her thoughts.

She nodded, and they fell into their familiar pattern. But this time, as

they threw the ball back and forth across the cinder lot, McGinty
understood what they were really doing. They were both practicing for
lives they might never fully achieve. She was practicing for a baseball
team that wouldn"t let her join. He was practicing for a fatherhood
that circumstances had taken away from him.

But they practiced anyway, because what else was there to do? Give up
entirely? Stop trying? That seemed worse than the constant striving, the
perpetual falling short.

One afternoon, when the fish store had closed and Rube was cleaning up,
McGinty sat on an overturned crate watching him work. He was hosing down
the wooden racks where the fish had been displayed, washing away the
slime and scales and debris of the day"s business. The work was
degrading, but Rube approached it with the same careful attention he
gave to everything else.

The fish store workers walked around him as if he were invisible, never
acknowledging his presence. They had gloves and rubber boots to protect
them from the mess. Rube had only the large rubber apron they"d given
him and his own worn shoes that were now soaked through with fish water.

But he didn"t complain. He just did the work, did it well, and

collected his small payment at the end. A few dollars and maybe a piece
of fish that hadn"t sold, wrapped in newspaper for his dinner.

McGinty thought about dignity, about how it could exist even in circumstances that seemed designed to strip it away. Rube had dignity.

It was there in the way he held himself, in the care he took with his appearance despite having nowhere to shower properly, in the love he
showed his son despite being unable to provide a home.

Her father had had dignity too, in his better moments. When he"d stood
a little straighter in his clean shirt before his first day at the parking lot. When he"d smiled at McGinty and called her his McGinty-girl. When he"d tried, even knowing he would probably fail.

The failing didn"t erase the trying. That"s what McGinty was beginning
to understand. Her father had failed, and he"d died because of it. But
he"d also tried, and that counted for something. It had to count for something, or else what was the point of any of it?

Rube finished his work and came over, stripping off the wet apron and
hanging it on a hook by the back door. His shirt underneath was damp
with sweat and fish water, but he didn"t seem bothered by it.

All done for today, he said. They want me back tomorrow morning to
unload a delivery. Early, before the store opens.

That"s good, McGinty said.

Yeah. Means I can give a little more to his mother next week. Maybe get

him a new jacket for winter.

They sat in comfortable silence for a while, watching the alley settle into evening. Other Bottle Babies were emerging from their daytime

hiding spots, preparing for another night of survival. Mossy was already

cooking something in his rusted can, the smell of whatever he was brewing drifting across the cinder path.

You"re a good father, McGinty said suddenly.

Rube looked at her, surprise written across his weathered face. I live in a cardboard box, Little Miss. I can"t even provide a roof over his head. How does that make me a good father?

Because you try, McGinty said simply. Because you save money for him

instead of spending it on drink. Because you show up, even when it"s

hard. That"s what good fathers do. They try.

Rube was quiet for a long moment, and when he spoke again, his voice was

thick with emotion. Your father was a good man too, you know. Whatever

else happened, whatever he struggled with, he loved you kids. He tried

his best, even when his best wasn"t enough.

McGinty felt tears prick at her eyes, but she blinked them back. I know.

I know he did.

They sat together as darkness fell over the alley, a seven-year-old girl and a homeless man, both understanding something about fathers and daughters and the complicated ways people tried to love each other despite their failures.

And in that understanding was a kind of grace, a recognition that human

beings were messy and broken and beautiful all at once, and that perhaps

the trying mattered more than anyone wanted to admit.

Chapter 5: The Butcher"'s Bargains

The Butcher"'s crutch made a distinctive sound on the cinders, a
rhythmic click-drag-step that announced his presence from blocks
away.

McGinty had learned to recognize it, to know when he was
approaching
even before she could see him. It was a lonely sound, she thought,
the
soundtrack of a man navigating the world with half his body
missing.

She watched from her back gate as he made his way up the alley
toward
the Avenue. His right pant leg was pinned up today, displaying the
absence of his lower leg. That meant he was going panhandling,
McGinty
realized. When he wasn"'t working panhandling duty, The Butcher
would
unpin the leg and attach the wooden prosthetic he kept hidden
somewhere
in his cardboard stash. With the prosthetic on, he looked almost
normal,
just a man with a slight limp. Without it, he looked pitiable, and
pitiable brought in more coins.

It was a calculated deception, this display of his disability. McGinty
understood that now. The Butcher had learned to weaponize his
injury, to
use people"'s sympathy to his advantage. Some might call it
dishonest,
but McGinty had started to see it as survival. When you had
nothing, you
used whatever tools you had.

Later that afternoon, The Butcher returned with the swagger of a
successful hunt. His pockets clinked with change, and he was
whistling a
tune McGinty didn"t recognize. He spotted her playing jacks on
the back
porch and altered his course to approach her.
Hey there, McGinty girl, he called up. Had yourself a good day?
McGinty nodded, scooping up her jacks. The Butcher dug in his
pocket and
pulled out two nickels, holding them out to her. His hand was
gnarled
and dirty, the fingernails black with grime, but the gesture was
genuine.
Here, he said. Go get yourself some penny candy or a picture show.
McGinty hesitated. She knew what her mother would say about
raking money
from The Butcher. But ten cents was ten cents, and ten cents could
buy
her admission to the Saturday matinee with enough left over for a
candy
bar.
She climbed down the porch steps and accepted the nickels, the
metal
warm from being in The Butcher"s pocket. Thank you.
The Butcher"s weathered face cracked into something that might
have
been a smile. You"re a good kid. Your dad, he used to look out for
me
sometimes. Figure I can return the favor to his girl.
The mention of her father made McGinty"s throat tight. She
nodded,

unable to speak, and The Butcher seemed to understand. He tapped his

crutch twice on the cinders in an awkward goodbye and hobbled off toward

his cardboard setup.

McGinty watched him go, thinking about what he"d said. Her father had

looked out for The Butcher. Not with grand gestures or charity checks,

but in the small ways that mattered to men living on the margins. A

cigarette shared. A warning about which cops were making sweeps. Maybe

even a couple of dollars when The Butcher was desperate.

The system of debts and favors in the alley was intricate, McGinty was

learning. Everyone owed everyone something, and everyone remembered.

When you had nothing, memory and obligation were the currencies that

kept the social structure intact.

A few days later, McGinty witnessed another side of The Butcher"s

business dealings. She was in the alley collecting returnable bottles

when she saw him engaged in a heated argument with Mossy. Their voices

rose and fell in angry waves, though McGinty couldn"t make out the

specific words from where she stood.

The Butcher was gesturing wildly with his free hand, his crutch planted

firmly as he leaned forward aggressively. Mossy stood his ground, his massive frame somehow made larger by his rage. For a moment, McGinty

thought they might come to blows, despite The Butcher"s obvious disadvantage.

Then Rube appeared, his large hands raised in a peacekeeping gesture. He

stepped between the two men, saying something in his deep, calm voice.

The tension broke like a snapped rubber band. The Butcher spat on the

ground but backed away. Mossy turned and disappeared into his cardboard

fortress, still muttering curses.

Rube caught McGinty"s eye and shook his head slightly, a warning to

stay back. She did, pressing herself against the wall of her house and

making herself small. Violence in the alley was rare but not unknown,

and when it happened, it was best to be invisible.

Later, when things had calmed down, McGinty asked Rube what the fight

had been about.

Same thing it"s always about with those two, Rube said with a sigh.

Mossy"s Sneaky Pete. The Butcher wanted some on credit, and Mossy

doesn"t give credit to nobody.

But The Butcher gives me nickels sometimes, McGinty said. Why doesn"t

he just buy the Sneaky Pete?

Rube"s expression was a mix of sadness and understanding. Because once

you start drinking in the morning, Little Miss, you don"t stop until the money"s gone or you pass out. The Butcher, he"s trying to hold onto some of what he makes. Trying to be smart about it. But the wanting, it doesn"t care about smart.

McGinty thought about her father, about the bottles hidden around the
house, about the morning drinking that had escalated until there was no
morning or night, just one continuous haze of alcohol. The wanting
didn"t care about smart. That made sense in a terrible way.

One evening, just before the fish market closed, McGinty saw The Butcher
engaged in a different kind of transaction. A delivery truck had unloaded crates of vegetables at the back door, and one crate of broccoli had split open, spilling its contents across the loading dock.

The fish market owner stood looking at the mess, clearly debating whether it was worth salvaging. The broccoli was wilted but not rotten,
still edible if you weren"t particular. The owner called to The Butcher, who"d been loitering nearby.

You want this? the owner asked, gesturing to the spilled vegetables. I"ll give you a dollar if you clean it up and take it away.

The Butcher nodded, already moving toward the crate. His movements were
practiced and efficient despite the crutch. Within minutes, he"d gathered the broccoli into a salvageable pile, separated the truly ruined pieces from those that were just bruised.

McGinty watched as The Butcher negotiated with the owner, his voice too
low for her to hear. Finally, the owner went inside and returned with

not just a dollar but also a large paper bag. The Butcher loaded the better pieces of broccoli into the bag, accepted his payment, and hobbled away.

To McGinty"s surprise, The Butcher came directly to her back gate. He

held out the bag of broccoli, his expression unreadable.

For your ma, he said. Tell her it"s fresh today, just came in. Ain"t nothing wrong with it that a good rinse won"t fix.

McGinty took the bag, feeling the weight of the vegetables inside. This

was real food, enough to feed her family for a meal or two. Why are you

giving this to us?

The Butcher shifted on his crutch, uncomfortable with the question. Your

dad did me favors. This is me paying back.

But you gave me nickels already, McGinty pointed out. And this is worth

more than that.

A man can owe more than one debt, The Butcher said gruffly. Besides,

what am I gonna do with all this broccoli? Can"t cook it over Mossy"s

fire without him wanting a cut. Better it goes to someone who can use it

proper.

McGinty carried the broccoli inside, where her mother received it with

surprised gratitude. That evening, they had boiled broccoli with butter

and salt, a green vegetable that wasn"t the hated kale. Her sisters

picked at it uncertainly, but McGinty ate every bite, thinking about The
Butcher and the complicated web of obligation that bound their lives
together.

Over the following weeks, McGinty began to understand The Butcher
better. He was harsh and often mean, quick to anger and quicker to curse. But he operated by a code, a system of reciprocity that made sense in the brutal economy of the alley.

She saw him help Jimmy one night when the frailer man was struggling to
move a particularly large piece of cardboard for his sleeping spot. The
Butcher, despite his own disability, maneuvered the cardboard with his
crutch and his good leg, getting it positioned where Jimmy needed it.

Jimmy, nervous and trembling as always, offered The Butcher a cigarette
in thanks. The Butcher took it without comment, and they smoked together
in silence, two damaged men sharing a moment of mutual support.

McGinty thought about her father"s lies. Not the big, dramatic lies,
but the small daily deceptions. Saying he hadn"t been drinking when the
smell of alcohol hung around him like cologne. Claiming he"d been at
the parking lot all day when Lefty had to cover for his absence.
Promising to come to her school play and then not showing up.

The Butcher lied too. He lied about his leg when he pinned up his pants

and begged for money. He lied about where he got food or how he"d

earned his coins. He lied about being completely drunk when he was only

halfway there, hiding his level of intoxication to avoid trouble with the cops.

But the lies were survival strategies, McGinty understood now. They

weren"t malicious or meant to hurt. They were the tools of people who"d been pushed to the margins, who"d learned that strict honesty

was a luxury they couldn"t afford.

Her father had lied to protect what little dignity he had left. To maintain the fiction that he was still in control, still capable, still the man he"d once been. The lies had been acts of desperation, not cruelty.

One Saturday afternoon, McGinty was sitting on her back porch when The

Butcher approached with an awkward gait. His face was bruised, his

knuckles scraped and bleeding. He"d been in a fight, clearly, though he

said nothing about it.

He held out a quarter this time, not nickels. Take it, he said. Get yourself something nice.

McGinty looked at his battered face, at the fresh blood seeping from his

knuckles. Are you okay?

The question seemed to startle him. His weathered features softened

slightly, and something like gratitude flickered in his eyes. I"m fine,
kid. Just had a disagreement with someone who needed disagreeing
with.

McGinty took the quarter but didn"t move to go inside. The
Butcher

noticed her hesitation and let out a long sigh.

Your ma ever tell you how I lost the leg? he asked suddenly.

McGinty shook her head.

War, The Butcher said. Same war as Mossy, different battle. Stepped
on

something that exploded, and when I woke up in the field hospital,
half

my leg was gone. They sent me home with a Purple Heart and a
pension

that don"t hardly buy enough to live on.

He looked down at his pinned-up pant leg, at the space where his
lower

leg should have been. Used to have a wife, too. Three kids. But she
couldn"t handle the drinking, and I couldn"t handle the
nightmares

without the drinking. So she took the kids and left, and the pension
went to child support, and here I am.

The admission hung in the air between them. McGinty understood
that this

was important, that The Butcher was trusting her with something
he

probably didn"t share often.

I"m sorry, she said simply.

The Butcher waved away her sympathy with his damaged hand.
Don"t be.

Life happens how it happens. You deal with it or you don"t. I"m
still

here, ain"t I? Still breathing, still fighting. That"s something.

He turned to leave but paused. Your dad, he knew about all that. Never

judged me for it. Just treated me like a person. That"s why I"m good

to you, McGinty girl. Because your dad was good to me when most people

weren"t.

McGinty watched The Butcher hobble away, his crutch clicking against the

cinders. She thought about his three children, wherever they were, and

wondered if they knew their father was alive. Wondered if they thought

about him, missed him, hated him for the drinking that had driven their

mother away.

She thought about how quickly life could change, how one explosion could

take away half your leg and eventually your entire family. How pain led

to drinking, and drinking led to more pain, and soon you were trapped in

a cycle that seemed impossible to break.

But The Butcher was still here, still surviving. Still finding ways to

be kind despite his circumstances, still operating by a code even if

that code was rough around the edges. He wasn"t a good man in the way

that Sunday school teachers talked about goodness. But he wasn"t

entirely bad either. He was complicated, broken, and trying in his own

way to make sense of a life that had gone terribly wrong.

Just like her father had been. Just like all of them were, these Bottle

Babies who lived in cardboard boxes and drank themselves into
oblivion
   each night. They were people, with histories and wounds and small
   moments of generosity that suggested the men they"d once been,
the men
   they might have remained if circumstances had been different.

Chapter 6: Jimmy''s Trembling World

The latch on the back gate clicked softly, and McGinty''s head snapped
up from where she sat on the concrete step. That sound meant only
one
thing. Jimmy.

She pressed her face against the screen door, watching as the thin
figure made his way slowly across the small yard. Even from here,
she
could see his hands shaking as he reached up to smooth down his
thinning
hair. Jimmy always did that before he knocked. Like he was
preparing
himself to be seen.

Three soft taps on the back door. So quiet McGinty wondered how
her
mother always heard them.

"Mrs.?" His voice came through the door, barely above a whisper.
"Mrs., do you have anything extra to eat?"

McGinty''s mother appeared from the kitchen, wiping her hands
on her
apron. She didn''t look surprised. She never did when Jimmy came
calling.

"Wait a minute here, Jimmy. I think I have something."

McGinty watched her mother disappear back into the kitchen.
Through the
doorway, she could see her pulling out the bread, unwrapping the
wax
paper from the baloney, spreading mustard carefully on each slice.
Two
sandwiches. Always two. One for now, one for later.

Her mother folded the sandwiches into fresh wax paper, then placed them

in a small brown paper bag. The bag was important. McGinty understood

that now, though she hadn"t at first. The bag meant Jimmy could put it

in his pocket. The bag meant it looked like he might have bought something, not begged for it. The bag meant dignity.

"Here you go, Jimmy."

Jimmy"s hands trembled as he took the bag. They always trembled. Sometimes worse than others, but always moving, always shaking like he

was cold even on the warmest days.

"Thank you, Mrs. Thank you so much. I appreciate it, I really do." He

clutched the bag to his chest, his thin fingers white at the knuckles.

"I"ll pay you back when I get some work. I will."

"Don"t worry about it, Jimmy. You take care now."

He nodded quickly, too many times, his whole body seeming to vibrate

with the motion. Then he turned and walked back across the yard, his

footsteps crunching softly on the patchy grass until he reached the gate. The latch clicked again, and he was gone up the alley.

McGinty"s mother stood at the door for a moment, watching him go. Her

face held that look McGinty had seen before. Sad but not pitying. Worried but not scared. Like she understood something McGinty was still

learning.

"Ma?" McGinty asked softly. "Why does Jimmy shake like that?"

Her mother sighed and sat down on the step beside her. For a long

moment, she didn"t say anything. Just looked out at the alley where
Jimmy had disappeared.

"Jimmy"s sick, sweetheart. He"s got something called nerves.
Makes

him shake and worry about everything. The drinking helps him feel
calm,

but then when he doesn"t drink, the shaking gets worse. It"s a
terrible thing."

"Like Daddy?"

Her mother"s jaw tightened. She nodded slowly. "Like Daddy.
Jimmy and

your father went to school together, you know. Down at Our Lady
of

Mercy. They were friends when they were boys."

McGinty tried to picture it. Jimmy and her father as boys in
matching

school uniforms, carrying books, playing in the schoolyard. It
seemed

impossible. Her father had been solid, real, present. Jimmy seemed
like

he might blow away in a strong wind.

"What happened to him?" McGinty asked.

"Life happened, I suppose. Jimmy went to the war. When he came
back, he

wasn"t the same. The nerves started then. He tried to work, but the
shaking made it hard. Then his mother died, and he had nobody to
help

him. That"s when the drinking got bad."

Her mother stood up, brushing off her dress. "But he"s not a bad
man,

McGinty. Don"t ever think that. Jimmy"s just someone who got
knocked

down and couldn"t get back up. Could happen to anybody."

McGinty thought about that as she watched the empty alley. Could happen

to anybody. Even her father. Even her.

'* '* '*

Two days later, McGinty saw Jimmy again. This time, he was outside The

Derby, sweeping the front steps with a broom that had seen better days.

Half the bristles were missing, but Jimmy worked methodically, carefully

pushing the cigarette butts and dirt into a neat pile.

His hands still shook, but he managed to control the broom well enough.

Sweat beaded on his forehead despite the cool morning air. Every few

sweeps, he"d pause and wipe his face with a handkerchief he kept in his

back pocket.

"Hey, Jimmy!" McGinty called out.

He looked up, startled, then relaxed when he saw it was her. A small smile crossed his thin face. "Morning, Little Miss. You doing okay?"

"Yeah. You working?"

"Yes, ma"am. Lefty"s got me doing some cleaning today. Dishes later

too." He said it with a note of pride, standing a little straighter.

Lefty appeared in the doorway, a thick-set man with slicked-back hair

and a gold watch that caught the sunlight. He had the kind of face that could look friendly or dangerous depending on his mood. Right now, he

was smiling.

"Jimmy, when you"re done with that, come inside. Got a sandwich and

coffee for you." Lefty"s eyes shifted to McGinty. "Morning, kid. Your

ma doing okay?"

"Yes, sir."

"Good. You tell her if she needs anything, she just has to ask. Your old man, he was a good guy. We look after our own."

Lefty disappeared back inside, and Jimmy resumed his sweeping with

renewed energy. McGinty sat down on the bottom step, careful to stay out

of his way.

"Jimmy? Did you know my dad when he was little?"

The broom paused. Jimmy leaned on it, his face softening with memory.

"Sure did. Your dad and me, we were in the same class from first grade

on. He was a good kid. Always helped the other boys who couldn"t keep

up. Shared his lunch with kids who didn"t have one."

"Really?"

"Really. Your dad, he had a good heart. When we got back from the war,

things were tough for both of us. But your dad, he got that parking lot

job. And you know what he did?"

McGinty shook her head.

"He went to Lefty and told him I needed work. Said I was reliable, said

I"d show up when I said I would. Lefty gave me a chance because your

dad vouched for me. That"s the kind of man your father was."

Jimmy"s voice cracked a little on the last words. He cleared his throat, went back to sweeping. "I owe your dad a lot. Wish I could have

done more for him when he got sick."

"You came to the funeral," McGinty said quietly. She remembered seeing

Jimmy there, standing in the back of the church, his hands clasped together to stop the shaking. He"d stayed for the whole service, then

slipped out before anyone could talk to him.

"Of course I did. Your dad was my friend. Best friend I ever had."

Jimmy looked down at his shaking hands, then quickly gripped the broom

handle tighter. "I know I"m not much to look at now. But your dad never made me feel small. Never made me feel like I was less than anybody else."

"I don"t think you"re small," McGinty said.

Jimmy smiled at her, and for just a moment, she could see the boy he

must have been. The friend her father had known. "You"re a good kid,

Little Miss. Just like your old man."

"* "* "*

That night, McGinty heard her mother talking to her older sister in the

kitchen. She wasn"t supposed to be listening, but she was good at being quiet when she wanted to be.

"I saw Jimmy today," her mother was saying. "He looked worse. Thinner. The shaking"s getting bad."

"Is he drinking again?"

"I don"t know. Maybe. Or maybe he"s trying not to and that"s why he"s shaking so bad. Either way, it"s not good."

Her sister sighed. "It"s sad. He used to be so different. Remember when he worked at the post office? Before the war?"

"I remember. He was always polite, always had his uniform pressed just

so. The war changed him. Changed a lot of men."

"Like Dad."

A long silence. Then her mother"s voice, quieter now. "Yes. Like your

father."

McGinty pressed herself against the wall, her heart beating hard. She"d

never heard her mother talk about her father"s drinking like this. Like

it was something that happened to him, not something he chose.

"At least Lefty looks after Jimmy," her sister said. "Gives him work when he can."

"Lefty"s a good man, in his way. He looked after your father too. Made

sure he had that parking lot job even when he couldn"t hardly stand up

straight some days. These men, they take care of each other. There"s honor in that, even if the priests wouldn"t see it that way."

McGinty crept away from the door and climbed the stairs to her room. She

lay in bed, thinking about Jimmy and her father. About Lefty and The

Derby. About how the world was more complicated than the nuns at school

made it seem.

Good men and bad men. But what about the men in between? The men who did

bad things but also took care of people? The men who were broken but

still tried? Where did they fit?

"* "* "*

A week passed before McGinty saw Jimmy again. This time, he was in the

alley near Mossy"s spot. McGinty watched from her back step as Jimmy

approached, his thin frame tense with visible anxiety.

"Mossy," Jimmy called out, his voice wavering. "Mossy, you got any Pete today?"

Mossy emerged from his cardboard kingdom, his leg wrappings crusted with

old blood and pus. He squinted at Jimmy through bleary eyes. "Got

money?"

Jimmy"s hand shook as he pulled out some coins. "I got a dime."

Mossy grunted, snatched the coins, and disappeared back into his lair.

He emerged with a small tin cup, sloshing with clear liquid. Jimmy took

it carefully, his whole body trembling now.

"Thanks, Mossy."

Jimmy lifted the cup to his lips and drank. McGinty watched his face

contort as the liquid went down. He coughed, wiped his mouth, then drank again. By the time the cup was empty, his hands had stopped shaking

quite so badly.

He stood there for a moment, breathing deeply, his eyes closed. When he

opened them, he looked steadier. More like himself. He handed the cup

back to Mossy and walked down the alley, his gait more confident now.

McGinty felt a twist in her stomach. The drinking made Jimmy worse. But

it also made him better. How could both things be true?

She thought about her father stumbling through the back door late at

night, her mother"s tight face, the whispered arguments. But she also

remembered him on good days, when he"d had just enough to stop the

shaking in his hands, when he"d smile and joke and act like the man he

used to be.

The medicine that was also poison.

'* '* '*

On Saturday afternoon, McGinty walked past The Derby on her way to the

corner store. Through the open door, she could hear men"s voices, the

clink of glasses, the scratch of a match being struck.

She peered inside. The place was dim, thick with cigarette smoke that

hung in the air like fog. Men sat at small tables, bent over racing forms and notepads. In the corner, Lefty stood behind the bar, pouring

drinks.

And there was Jimmy, washing glasses in a small sink behind the bar. His

sleeves were rolled up, and his thin arms worked steadily despite the

tremor. Steam rose from the hot water, and his face was flushed from the

heat.

Lefty saw her in the doorway and waved her in. "Come here, kid. Don"t

stand out there like a stranger."

McGinty stepped inside, her eyes adjusting to the gloom. The smell of

beer and cigarettes was overwhelming, but underneath it was something

else. Coffee. Someone was making coffee.

"Jimmy"s doing good work today," Lefty said, loud enough for Jimmy to

hear. "Real good work. Best dishwasher I got."

Jimmy looked up from the sink, his face breaking into a shy smile.

"Thank you, boss."

"You hungry, kid?" Lefty asked McGinty.

She shook her head, though she was always a little hungry.

"Don"t lie to me. I can hear your stomach from here." Lefty reached

under the bar and pulled out a wrapped sandwich. "Take it. And don"t

tell your ma I"m feeding you in a bar. She"ll have my head."

McGinty took the sandwich, warm in her hands. "Thank you, Mr. Lefty."

"Just Lefty. Nobody calls me mister." He turned back to Jimmy. "When

you"re done with those, take a break. Got a plate of spaghetti for you

in the back."

Jimmy"s hands, still in the soapy water, stilled for a moment. "Spaghetti?"

"Yeah, spaghetti. What, you deaf? Go on, finish up."

McGinty watched Jimmy scrub the last glass, rinse it, and set it carefully on the drying rack. He dried his hands on a towel, then disappeared through a door at the back of the bar.

"Is Jimmy okay?" McGinty asked Lefty.

Lefty leaned against the bar, his thick arms crossed. "Jimmy? Yeah, he"s okay. He"s got his troubles, but we all do. He shows up when he

says he will. He works hard. That"s all I ask."

"My dad helped him get this job."

"Your dad was smart. He knew Jimmy needed something to hang onto. A

reason to get up in the morning. Work does that for a man. Gives him

purpose."

Lefty looked at her for a long moment, his face serious. "Your old man,

he understood that because he needed it too. That parking lot job, it

kept him going longer than he would have otherwise. Gave him something

to be proud of."

McGinty felt tears prick at her eyes. She blinked them back hard.

"You"re a tough kid," Lefty said quietly. "Just like him. Now go on, get out of here. This ain"t a place for little girls."

But his voice was kind, and when McGinty turned to leave, he called

after her. "Hey, kid. You need anything, you come see me. Understand?

Anything at all."

McGinty nodded and stepped back out into the bright sunlight, clutching

her sandwich.

'* '* '*

Two weeks later, Jimmy came to the back door again. This time, McGinty

answered it.

He stood on the step, his clothes cleaner than usual, his hair combed

back. His hands still shook, but not as badly as before.

"Is your ma home, Little Miss?"

"She"s in the kitchen. You want sandwiches?"

Jimmy smiled. "No, actually. I wanted to give her something."

He pulled out a small envelope from his jacket pocket. His hands trembled as he held it out. "Could you give this to her? It"s not much, but I"ve been working steady at The Derby for three weeks now. I

wanted to pay her back for all those sandwiches."

McGinty took the envelope carefully. It felt light, but the gesture felt

heavy.

"She"ll say you don"t have to," McGinty told him.

"I know. But I do have to. Your ma showed me kindness when I had nothing. Your dad did too. I can"t ever repay that fully, but I can do this much."

Jimmy straightened up, looking her in the eye. For just a moment, she could see the man he might have been without the nerves, without the

alcohol, without the war. A decent man. A good friend.

"You take care, Little Miss. You"re going to be okay. I can tell. You got your dad"s heart."

He turned and walked back through the gate, his footsteps steady on the

path. McGinty watched him go, the envelope still in her hand.

When she gave it to her mother, she watched her open it. Inside were

three dollar bills. Her mother"s eyes filled with tears.

"That"s probably everything he has," her mother whispered. "That"s

probably his whole pay for the week."

"He wanted to give it to you," McGinty said. "He said it was important."

Her mother folded the bills carefully and put them in her apron pocket.

"Jimmy"s got more dignity in his little finger than most men have in

their whole bodies. People see a drunk, a bum. But I see a man trying

his best with what he"s got."

She looked at McGinty. "Don"t ever forget that, sweetheart. Don"t ever judge people by what they look like on the outside. You look at

what"s inside. At the heart. That"s what matters."

McGinty nodded. She thought about Jimmy"s trembling hands carefully

washing glasses. About him standing straight when Lefty complimented his work. About him scraping together three dollars just to pay back a debt

of sandwiches.

People took care of each other. In whatever way they could. With sandwiches in paper bags. With work that gave purpose. With friendship

that survived everything.

That night, McGinty heard the latch on the gate click again. She looked

out her window and saw Jimmy walking down the alley, his shoulders back,

his stride confident. He was headed toward The Derby, where Lefty would

have work for him tomorrow.

And for tonight, that was enough.

Chapter 7: The Derby and the Bookies

The Derby sat on the corner like a squat guardian, its brick face
    weathered by decades of city soot and rain. To most people passing
by,
    it looked like any other neighborhood bar. A neon sign flickered in
the
    window advertising beer. Dark curtains blocked the view inside.
Nothing
    special.

But McGinty knew better. Everyone in the neighborhood knew
better.

The Derby was where Lefty and his crew ran their business.
Numbers,
    horses, football games. Money changed hands in quiet corners.
Bets were
    placed with whispered codes. And the men who worked there, the
men who
    protected it, they were the ones who really kept the neighborhood
    running.

McGinty"s father had worked for them. First at the parking lot
they
    owned, then doing odd jobs when his health got worse. Even after
he
    couldn"t stand for full shifts, they kept finding him work. Small
    things. Watching a doorway. Delivering packages. Enough to keep
some
    money coming in.

"They looked after him," her mother had said once, her voice tight
    with complicated feelings. "God help me, those men looked after
your
    father better than some of our own family did."

McGinty understood what she meant. The uncle who stopped visiting when

her father"s drinking got bad. The cousins who crossed the street to avoid them. The neighbors who whispered behind their hands.

But Lefty? Lefty kept her father working. Kept him feeling like a man.

"* "* "*

McGinty remembered the day they came to the house after her father died.

She"d been sitting on the front steps, her mother inside with relatives

who kept crying and saying useless things like "He"s in a better place

now" and "At least he"s not suffering anymore."

A black Cadillac pulled up to the curb. Shiny, clean, looking out of place on their shabby street. Three men got out, all wearing dark suits

despite the summer heat. Lefty was in the middle, flanked by two others

McGinty didn"t know as well.

They walked up to the house with the kind of confidence that came from

owning the neighborhood. But when Lefty saw McGinty on the steps, his

hard face softened just a little.

"Hey, kid. Your ma inside?"

McGinty nodded, unable to find her voice.

"We just want to pay our respects. Your old man, he was good people."

Lefty reached into his jacket and pulled out an envelope. Thick. White.

He crouched down so he was eye-level with McGinty. This close, she could

smell his cologne and see the small scar above his left eyebrow.

"Give this to your mother. Tell her it"s from all of us at The Derby. For expenses."

McGinty took the envelope with both hands. It felt heavy. Important.

"And tell her this," Lefty continued, his voice low and serious.

"Tell her if she needs anything, anything at all, she comes to see me. The rent gets tough? She comes to see me. The kids need school clothes?

She comes to see me. Understand?"

"Yes, sir."

Lefty stood up, adjusting his tie. "Your dad was a stand-up guy. Worked

hard, kept his mouth shut, never complained. We don"t forget that."

The three men went inside for ten minutes. McGinty could hear low

voices, her mother"s tear-choked thank you, the shuffle of feet on the

worn carpet. When they came back out, they nodded to her and got back in

the Cadillac.

Later, her mother opened the envelope. Five hundred dollars. More money

than McGinty had ever seen at once. Her mother sat at the kitchen table

and cried, the bills spread out in front of her.

"God forgive me," she whispered. "But these men have been kinder to

us than the church ever was."

'* '* '*

McGinty started paying more attention to The Derby after that. She"d

watch the men coming and going. Regulars who showed up every afternoon

with their racing forms. Others who slipped in through the side door,

stayed for ten minutes, then left with their hands in their pockets.

She learned the rhythms of the place. Quiet in the mornings when Rube or

Jimmy cleaned the brass and swept the floors. Busier in the afternoons

when men came to place their bets. Loudest in the evenings when the

races were over and people celebrated wins or drowned their losses.

One afternoon, she saw something that made her understand the place

better. She was walking past The Derby when a commotion started down the

street. Two men were arguing, their voices rising. One shoved the other.

People on the sidewalk backed away.

Before the fight could really start, Lefty came out of The Derby. He

didn"t run. Didn"t shout. Just walked up to the two men with his hands

in his pockets, calm as could be.

"Hey. Hey!" His voice cut through the noise like a knife. "What"s going on here?"

The two men stopped mid-shove. The one who"d been winning suddenly

looked nervous. "Nothing, Lefty. Just a disagreement."

"A disagreement. In front of my place?" Lefty looked at each man in

turn. "You two know the rules. No fighting on this block. You got a

problem, you take it somewhere else. Or you come inside and we settle it

civilized."

"Sorry, Lefty. We"re done here."

The two men separated, walking in opposite directions. The crowd that

had gathered started to disperse. Lefty stood there for another minute,

making sure things stayed calm, then went back inside.

McGinty watched it all from across the street. She understood then that

The Derby wasn"t just a bar. It was power. Protection. Order. Lefty

kept the peace not because he was good, but because chaos was bad for

business. And somehow, that made everyone safer.

"* "* "*

She started noticing other things too. How Rube would show up on

Saturdays to polish the brass railings and clean the windows. How he"d

leave with cash in his pocket and food wrapped in newspaper. How Lefty

would clap him on the shoulder and call him reliable.

One Saturday, McGinty gathered her courage and went inside. The door was

heavy, and she had to use both hands to push it open. Inside, it took a

moment for her eyes to adjust to the dim light.

The bar ran along the left wall, dark wood polished to a shine. Small
tables filled the space, most of them occupied by men hunched over
newspapers. A radio played quietly in the corner, announcing race
results. The air was thick with smoke and the smell of beer.

Rube was behind the bar, stacking clean glasses. When he saw
McGinty,
his face broke into a smile. "Little Miss! What are you doing in
here?"

Before she could answer, Lefty appeared from a back room. "I told
you,
kid. This ain"t a place for little girls."

But he was smiling. "What do you need?"

"I wanted to say thank you. For the money. For helping my family."

Lefty"s expression softened. He came around the bar and crouched
down
to her level, just like he had on her front steps. "You don"t need to
thank me, kid. Your father earned every penny of that and more.
He
worked hard for us. We take care of our own."

"But you"re'..." McGinty hesitated, not sure how to say it. "People
say you"re bad men."

Lefty laughed, a short bark that held no humor. "Bad men. Yeah, I
suppose we are. We break the law. We take bets. We make money
the
priests don"t approve of." He looked at her seriously. "But we also
keep this neighborhood safe. We make sure nobody comes in here
causing
trouble. We give men like your father and Jimmy and Rube jobs
when
nobody else will."

He stood up, straightening his jacket. "The world ain"t black and white, kid. Good men do bad things. Bad men do good things. You"ll

learn that as you get older."

From behind the bar, Rube called out, "Lefty"s got a code. We all do.

You don"t steal from the neighborhood. You don"t hurt women or kids.

You look after your people. That"s the code."

Lefty nodded. "That"s right. And your dad, he understood that code. He

lived by it. That"s why we respected him."

McGinty felt something shift inside her. A piece of understanding clicking into place. Her father had been part of this world. Not the churchgoing, respectable world her mother tried to maintain. But this

other world, with its own rules and its own honor.

"Now go on," Lefty said gently. "Get out of here before your ma finds

out you"ve been in a bookie joint. She"ll have both our heads."

'* '* '*

That night at dinner, McGinty"s mother mentioned that Mrs. O"Malley

from down the street had been complaining about The Derby again. "Says

it attracts the wrong element. Says it makes the neighborhood look bad."

McGinty"s older sister snorted. "Mrs. O"Malley"s son steals from the

corner store. But she"s worried about The Derby?"

"That"s enough," their mother said, but without much force behind it.

She looked tired, the lines around her eyes deeper than they used to be.

"I know what that place is. I know what goes on there. But'..."

She set down her fork. "But those men have been good to us. Better than

most. When your father was dying, when he couldn"t work anymore, they

kept finding him things to do. Kept his pride intact. And after he died,

they made sure we were taken care of."

She looked at McGinty, then at her sister. "Life isn"t as simple as

the nuns make it sound. Sometimes the people who are supposed to help

you don"t. And sometimes the people you"re supposed to stay away from

are the ones who show up when you need them."

McGinty thought about that later, lying in bed. She thought about Lefty

stopping the fight on the street. About Rube getting steady work that

let him support his son. About Jimmy being given a chance despite his

shaking hands. About her father having purpose in his last months because The Derby gave him jobs.

Bad men doing good things.

'* '* '*

A few weeks later, McGinty saw something that made her understand even

more. She was sitting on her back step when she heard raised voices from

the alley. Angry voices. Threatening.

She crept to the gate and peered through the slats. Two men she didn"t

recognize had cornered The Butcher near Mossy"s spot. One was holding

The Butcher"s crutch, keeping it just out of reach. The other was going

through The Butcher"s pockets.

"Come on, old man. You got money from panhandling. Hand it over."

The Butcher tried to hop away, but without his crutch, he couldn"t get

far. "I ain"t got nothing. Leave me alone."

The man laughed and pulled out a few coins from The Butcher"s pocket.

"This all you got? Pathetic."

McGinty"s heart pounded. She should get her mother. But before she

could move, she heard heavy footsteps coming up the alley. Fast. Purposeful.

Two men from The Derby appeared. She recognized them from seeing them

outside the bar. Big men. The kind who made space when they walked.

"What"s going on here?" The taller one"s voice was calm but held an

edge that made McGinty"s spine tingle.

The two thieves froze. "Nothing. Just talking to our friend here."

"Doesn"t look like talking. Looks like stealing. And that"s not allowed in this neighborhood."

"We didn"t know this was your territory."

"Now you do. Give the man his money back. And his crutch. Then get out of here and don"t come back."

The coins clinked as they hit the ground near The Butcher"s feet. The

crutch clattered beside them. The two thieves backed away, then turned

and ran.

One of The Derby men helped The Butcher retrieve his crutch and money.

"You okay?"

The Butcher nodded, still shaken. "Yeah. Thanks."

"You see anyone else causing trouble, you come find us. Lefty don"t like people messing with the neighborhood."

The men walked back toward The Derby, their job done. The Butcher stood

there for a moment, then hobbled over to Mossy"s spot and sat down

heavily.

McGinty stayed at the gate, processing what she"d seen. The Derby men

had protected The Butcher. A man who most people saw as trash, not worth

noticing. But in this neighborhood, he was under The Derby"s protection. He belonged.

They all did. Mossy and The Butcher and Jimmy and Rube. The Bottle

Babies were part of the neighborhood, and The Derby protected the

neighborhood.

"* "* "*

Later that week, McGinty"s mother sent her to the corner store. On the way back, she saw Lefty standing outside The Derby, smoking a cigarette.

He saw her and waved her over.

"How"s your ma doing?"

"She"s okay. Working a lot."

Lefty nodded. "She"s a strong woman. Your dad knew that. Used to talk

about her all the time. How proud he was that she kept the family together."

McGinty"s throat tightened. "Did my dad talk about me?"

"Are you kidding? All the time. You were his pride and joy, kid. He"d

tell anyone who"d listen about his smart daughter. How you were going

to make something of yourself." Lefty took a drag on his cigarette.

"He wanted better for you than what he had. That"s what every father

wants."

"I miss him."

"I know you do. We all do. Your dad was good people. One of the best I

ever worked with." Lefty dropped his cigarette and ground it out with

his shoe. "Listen, you remember what I told you. Your family needs anything, you come to me. That"s not charity. That"s taking care of our own. Your dad would do the same if the situation was reversed."

"Okay."

"And another thing." Lefty looked down at her seriously. "You"re going to hear people say bad things about your father. About his drinking. About where he worked. Don"t listen to them. Your father was

a man who did the best he could with what he had. He worked hard. He
loved his family. He had honor. That"s all that matters."
McGinty felt tears prick at her eyes but blinked them back. "Thank you,
Mr. Lefty."
"Just Lefty. Now get home before your ma worries."
McGinty walked home with her bag of groceries, thinking about her
father. About how he"d found his place in this complicated world. How
he"d been respected by men like Lefty. How he"d lived by a code that
wasn"t written down but was real nonetheless.
The Derby wasn"t a church. The men who ran it weren"t saints. But they
looked after their own. They kept the neighborhood safe. They gave dignity to men who had none left.
Bad men doing good things. Good men doing bad things. Maybe Lefty was
right. Maybe the world wasn"t black and white.
Maybe it was just people trying to survive, trying to take care of each
other in whatever way they could. And maybe that was enough.

Chapter 8: The Winter of Understanding

The first snow came early that year, in late November. McGinty woke up

to find the alley covered in white, the cinders and dirt hidden under a

clean blanket. It looked beautiful from her window. Peaceful.

But as she got dressed, pulling on her thick socks and the sweater her

mother had mended three times, all she could think about was the Bottle

Babies. Where would they go when it got cold? How would they stay warm?

At breakfast, she asked her mother. "Ma, what happens to Mossy and The

Butcher when it snows?"

Her mother looked up from the oatmeal she was stirring. "They manage.

Somehow they always do. Get more cardboard, layer it up. The store

owners let them stay in the doorways as long as they don"t cause trouble."

"But it"s cold, Ma. Really cold."

Her mother"s face softened. "I know, sweetheart. It"s a hard life they"ve got. But there"s not much we can do about it. We"re barely getting by ourselves."

McGinty ate her oatmeal in silence, but her mind was working. There had

to be something she could do. Something small.

ʻ* ʻ* ʻ*

That afternoon, McGinty started collecting cardboard. When she saw boxes

90

behind the grocery store, she dragged them down the alley. When the

butcher threw out the crates meat came in, she asked if she could have

them. He looked at her suspiciously but handed them over.

She stacked the cardboard near the back entrance of the bicycle shop,

not too close to Mossy"s spot but close enough that he"d find it. Then

she waited, watching from her back step.

Sure enough, Mossy came out of his cardboard fortress that evening,

grumbling and spitting as usual. He spotted the new boxes and stopped.

For a long moment, he just stood there, swaying slightly, looking at them.

Then he moved. Faster than McGinty had seen him move in months. He

grabbed the boxes and dragged them back to his spot, layering them over

his existing fortress. Making it thicker. Warmer.

McGinty smiled. It wasn"t much, but it was something.

The next day, she took it further. Her mother had made too much dinner,

a rare thing. McGinty asked if she could have the leftovers for lunch tomorrow.

"Sure, honey. Put them in the icebox."

But McGinty didn"t put them in the icebox. That night, when everyone

was asleep, she crept downstairs and wrapped the meatloaf and potatoes

in wax paper. Then she slipped out the back door.

The alley was dark and cold, her breath making clouds in the frigid
air.

She walked carefully on the icy cinders, holding the package tight
to

her chest.

Mossy"s spot was quiet. She could hear snoring from inside the

cardboard. She placed the package near the entrance where he"d
see it

in the morning, then hurried back to the house before anyone
noticed she

was gone.

'* '* '*

December came, and with it came bitter cold. The kind that made
your

nose hairs freeze when you breathed. The kind that made your
fingers

ache even inside gloves.

McGinty kept leaving food. Small things. A sandwich. Half an
apple.

Whatever she could sneak without her mother noticing. She never
saw

Mossy take the packages, but they were always gone by morning.

She did the same for The Butcher, leaving packages near the loading
dock

where he sometimes slept. And for Jimmy, tucking them under a
loose

board near The Derby"s back door where he"d find them.

It felt like a secret mission. Like she was a spy helping resistance
fighters. It made her feel useful. Important.

Then one morning, everything changed.

'* '* '*

McGinty was getting ready for school when she heard shouting from the

alley. Not angry shouting. Scared shouting.

She ran to the back door and looked out. Jimmy was in the alley, his

arms waving, his voice high and panicked. "Help! Someone help! Rube"s

sick! He won"t wake up!"

McGinty"s heart dropped into her stomach. She ran out without her coat,

her mother calling after her.

Rube was lying near The Derby"s back entrance, curled on his side. Even

from a distance, McGinty could see he was shaking, but not the normal

tremors she was used to. These were full-body shakes, violent and uncontrollable.

"Rube!" She ran to him and dropped to her knees. His face was gray,

his lips almost blue. When she touched his arm, he was burning up despite the cold.

"He"s been coughing for days," Jimmy said, his voice breaking. "But

this morning I found him like this. He"s real sick, Little Miss. Real sick."

McGinty"s mother appeared, her face tight with concern. She knelt

beside Rube and put her hand on his forehead. "He"s got fever. Bad fever. Jimmy, go get Lefty. Right now."

Jimmy ran toward The Derby, stumbling in his haste. McGinty stayed with

Rube, holding his massive hand in hers. It was hot and dry, and she could feel his pulse racing.

"Please don"t die," she whispered. "Please, Rube. Don"t die like my dad did."

Rube"s eyes fluttered open for just a second. He looked at her but didn"t seem to see her. Then his eyes closed again and his breathing got worse, raspy and wet sounding.

Lefty came running out of The Derby, his jacket open, his face serious.

Behind him came two other men. They took in the scene with quick,

professional glances.

"Pneumonia," Lefty said. "Got to be. In this cold, living like

this"..." He looked at one of his men. "Go call Doc Marino. Tell him it"s an emergency and I"m paying. Tell him to get here now."

The man ran back inside. Lefty crouched down next to Rube. "Hang on,

big guy. Doc"s coming. You"re gonna be okay."

McGinty"s mother put her arm around McGinty"s shoulders. "Come on,

honey. Let the men handle this."

"No!" McGinty pulled away. "I"m staying with Rube. He"s my friend."

Lefty looked at her, then nodded. "Let her stay. Rube would want her

here."

They waited. McGinty held Rube"s hand and talked to him, telling him

about playing catch, about how he was the best baseball player she knew,

about how his son needed him to get better. She didn"t know if he could

hear her, but she kept talking anyway.

Fifteen minutes later, a car pulled up. An older man with a black bag
got out and hurried over. He knelt beside Rube and opened his bag, pulling out a stethoscope.

"Pneumonia, like you said," Doc Marino confirmed after listening to
Rube"s chest. "He needs to be somewhere warm. Needs medicine. And he
needs it now, or he"s not going to make it."

"What do we do?" Lefty asked.

"Hospital would be best, but"..." The doctor looked at Rube"s ragged
clothes, his dirty skin. "They won"t take good care of him. You know
how they treat men like this."

Lefty"s jaw tightened. "Then we handle it ourselves. You tell me what
he needs, I"ll get it. He can stay in the back room at The Derby. We"ll keep him warm."

"Penicillin. Fluids. Rest. Someone needs to watch him day and night."

The doctor pulled out a pad and started writing. "I"ll come back twice
a day to check on him. But you need to keep him warm and hydrated.
That"s critical."

"Done." Lefty turned to his men. "Get him inside. Gentle. Jimmy, you"re on first watch. I"ll take over tonight."

They lifted Rube carefully and carried him into The Derby. McGinty
followed, ignoring her mother"s protests. She had to see where they were taking him.

The back room was small but warm. They laid Rube on a cot and piled

blankets over him. Someone brought a bucket of water and cloths for his

fever. Jimmy sat in a chair beside the cot, his hands still shaking but his face determined.

"I"ll watch him, boss. I won"t leave him."

"I know you won"t, Jimmy." Lefty put his hand on Jimmy"s shoulder.

"You"re a good friend."

'* '* '*

McGinty couldn"t concentrate at school that day. All she could think

about was Rube lying in that back room, fighting for his life. When the

final bell rang, she ran home faster than she ever had before.

Her mother was in the kitchen, and there was a pot of soup on the stove.

Good soup, with chicken and vegetables. Not the watery kind they usually

ate.

"Ma? What"s that for?"

"For Rube. Lefty sent word that he needs soup. Something nourishing. So

I"m making soup." Her mother stirred the pot, her face set in determination. "We don"t have much, but we have this. And Rube needs

it more than we do."

McGinty felt her throat tighten. "Is he going to be okay?"

"I don"t know, sweetheart. But he"s got a chance now. Thanks to Lefty and the doctor and everyone helping. That"s all anyone can ask for. A

chance."

When the soup was done, McGinty carried it to The Derby in a covered

pot, walking carefully so she wouldn"t spill a drop. Lefty met her at the door.

"Your ma made this?"

"Yes, sir. She said Rube needs it."

Lefty took the pot, his expression softer than usual. "Your ma"s a good woman. Tell her I said thank you."

"Can I see him? Just for a minute?"

Lefty hesitated, then nodded. "One minute. He"s sleeping, and he needs

his rest."

McGinty followed him to the back room. Rube was lying under a mountain

of blankets, his face still gray but not quite as gray as before. His breathing sounded a little easier. Jimmy was still in the chair beside him, but now The Butcher was there too, sitting in the corner.

"We"re taking shifts," The Butcher explained. "Jimmy, me, Lefty, a couple of the other guys. Someone"s with him all the time."

McGinty walked to the cot and looked down at Rube. He looked so much

smaller lying down. So vulnerable. She reached out and touched his hand

gently.

"You have to get better, Rube. You have to. Your son needs you. And I

need you. We"re supposed to play catch in the spring, remember?"

For just a second, she thought she felt his hand squeeze hers. Maybe it was her imagination. Maybe not.

'* '* '*

Over the next week, the whole neighborhood rallied. McGinty"s mother

kept making soup. The Chinese restaurant sent down hot tea and broth.

Someone donated extra blankets. The doctor came twice a day, just like

he promised.

And slowly, gradually, Rube got better.

The fever broke on the fourth day. McGinty heard about it from Jimmy,

who came to the back door with tears in his eyes. "He opened his eyes,

Little Miss. He knew who I was. He asked for water."

McGinty wanted to run to The Derby right then, but her mother held her

back. "Let him rest. He"s not strong yet. You can see him when he"s a

bit better."

Two days later, Lefty came to the house himself. He stood at the back

door, hat in hand, looking almost uncomfortable. "Your girl wanted to

see Rube. He"s asking for her. If it"s okay with you, Mrs., I"ll walk her over and bring her right back."

McGinty"s mother nodded. "Take care of her."

"With my life."

McGinty walked with Lefty down the alley, her heart pounding with .

anticipation. When they got to the back room, Rube was sitting up in bed, propped up with pillows. He looked thin and weak, but his eyes were

clear.

"Little Miss," he said, his voice hoarse but warm. "Come here."

McGinty ran to him and hugged him carefully, afraid he might break. Rube

wrapped his big arms around her and held on tight.

"They tell me you"ve been leaving food for us," he said quietly.

"You and your ma both."

McGinty pulled back, surprised. "How did you know?"

"Mossy told me. Said someone"s been leaving packages near his spot.

Said he figured it was you because the wax paper was the same kind your

ma uses." Rube smiled. "That was a kind thing you did. A real kind thing."

"I didn"t want you to be cold. Or hungry."

"I know. And it helped. More than you know." Rube"s eyes got shiny.

"You"re just like your dad. He was always looking out for people too.

Always trying to help."

"I miss him."

"I know you do. I miss him too. But he"d be real proud of you, Little

Miss. Real proud of the person you"re becoming."

They sat together for a while, not saying much. Just being there.

Finally, Lefty said it was time to go. McGinty hugged Rube one more

time.

"You"re going to get all the way better, right? So we can play catch?"

"You bet, Little Miss. Come spring, I"ll be ready. And this time, I promise I won"t throw so hard."

'* '* '*

The most surprising thing happened the next day. McGinty was in the

alley when she heard raised voices near Rube"s old spot by the fish store. She crept closer and peered around the corner.

Mossy was there, standing guard over a pile of Rube"s belongings. His

few tools, his spare clothes, his baseball mitt. And some kids from a

few blocks over were trying to take them.

"Get away from there!" Mossy growled, waving a piece of wood threateningly. "That"s Rube"s stuff! You don"t touch it!"

"What do you care, old man? He"s probably dead anyway."

Mossy"s face turned purple with rage. "He ain"t dead! And you ain"t

taking his things! Now get out of here before I crack your heads!"

The kids backed off, laughing nervously. Mossy stood there, breathing

hard, until they were gone. Then he carefully rearranged Rube"s belongings and covered them with a piece of tarp to keep them dry.

McGinty watched, her eyes wide. Mossy was protecting Rube"s stuff.

Mossy, who never shared anything, who chased people away from his

territory, was standing guard over his friend"s possessions.

She walked over slowly. Mossy saw her and grunted but didn"t chase her

away.

"That was nice of you," McGinty said. "Protecting Rube"s things."

Mossy spat to the side. "Rube"s a good guy. Ain"t many good guys left. Can"t let punks steal from him while he"s laid up."

It was the most coherent sentence McGinty had ever heard from Mossy. She

looked at him with new eyes. Under all that dirt and anger and sickness,

there was still a person. Still someone who cared about his friends.

"Thank you for the food," Mossy said suddenly, not looking at her.

"The packages. I know it was you."

McGinty didn"t know what to say. She just nodded.

"Your old man, he used to give me cigarettes sometimes. When he had

extra. Never said nothing about it. Just handed them over." Mossy finally looked at her, his rheumy eyes somehow sad. "You"re like him.

Good people."

Then he turned and shuffled back to his cardboard fortress, leaving McGinty standing there with tears in her eyes.

'* '* '*

That night, lying in bed, McGinty thought about everything that had

happened. How the whole neighborhood had come together for Rube. Lefty

paying for the doctor. Her mother making soup. The Chinese restaurant

sending food. Jimmy and The Butcher and even Mossy taking care of him.

When her father had been sick, some people had helped. Her mother"s

sister brought groceries. Lefty kept finding him work. Jimmy visited

when he could.

But others hadn"t. The relatives who stopped coming around. The neighbors who looked the other way. The people at church who whispered

but never offered real help.

The people who helped weren"t always the ones you"d expect. Sometimes

they were bookies and drunks and men living in cardboard boxes.

Sometimes kindness came from the strangest places.

And sometimes the people who should help, the respectable people, the

churchgoing people, were nowhere to be found when you needed them most.

McGinty understood something then, something important. The world was

complicated. People were complicated. And you couldn"t judge someone by

what they looked like or where they slept or how they made their living.

You judged them by how they treated people when it mattered. By whether

they showed up when someone needed help. By whether they protected their

friends and looked after their own.

By those measures, Lefty and Rube and even Mossy were better men than a

lot of people who wore suits and sat in church pews every Sunday.

Her father had known that. Had lived by that. And now McGinty was

starting to understand it too.

Outside, snow fell softly in the alley. But inside their cardboard fortresses and back rooms and borrowed beds, the Bottle Babies were

warm. Protected. Cared for.

Not because the world was kind. But because they took care of each other.

And that, McGinty realized, was what mattered most.

Chapter 9: The Painter Incident

Spring was trying to arrive, but winter kept hanging on with cold
fingers. The snow had melted, leaving behind dirty puddles and
exposed
trash that had been hidden under white blankets. The alley smelled
of
wet cinders and garbage.

McGinty was playing in the back yard, bouncing a rubber ball
against the
brick wall of the house next door. The Kowalskis" house was being
painted, finally, after years of peeling paint and exposed wood. A
man
had been working on it for three days now, his ladder propped
against
the side, paint cans scattered on the ground.

The painter was young, maybe thirty, with slicked-back hair and
rolled-up sleeves. He looked normal. Respectable. Clean. The kind
of man
mothers would point to and say, "That"s a working man. That"s
what
you want to be."

Mrs. Kowalski had a baby, not even a year old yet. Little Thomas.

McGinty had seen her carrying him around, cooing at him,
showing him off
to the neighbors. A good baby, everyone said. Quiet. Well-behaved.

That afternoon, Mrs. Kowalski had gone to the store, leaving the
baby
inside with the door open so the painter could hear if he cried. It
was
a warm day, one of the first real warm days, and the fresh air felt
good

after the long winter.

McGinty was bouncing her ball when she heard it. A slap. Sharp and loud.

Then a baby"s cry, suddenly cut off.

She froze, her ball rolling away across the patchy grass. Through the open window, she could see the painter. He was inside the house, standing over the baby"s crib. And as she watched, horrified, he raised his hand and hit the baby again.

"Shut up!" His voice was harsh, angry. "Shut your mouth, you little'..."

The words that followed made McGinty"s stomach turn. Words she"d heard in the alley sometimes, from the worst of the drunks. But never directed at a baby. Never at something so small and helpless.

The baby was crying now, wailing, and the painter shook the crib hard.

"I said shut up!"

McGinty stood there, paralyzed. She should do something. She should run.

She should yell. But her feet wouldn"t move and her voice wouldn"t work.

The painter turned and saw her watching through the window. His face changed, twisted into something ugly. He came to the window and leaned out.

"You didn"t see nothing, you hear me? Nothing. Or I"ll do the same to you, you little—-"

Another word. Another bad word that made McGinty feel dirty just hearing

it.

Then her feet remembered how to work. She turned and ran toward the

alley, her heart pounding so hard she thought it might burst out of her

chest.

'* '* '*

She found Rube near the fish store. He was back to work now, recovered

from his bout with pneumonia, though he still looked thinner than

before. He was stacking crates, his massive arms making the work look

easy despite his recent illness.

When he saw McGinty running toward him, tears streaming down her face,

he dropped the crate he was holding.

"Little Miss! What"s wrong? What happened?"

The words came tumbling out. The baby crying. The painter hitting him.

The awful words. The threat.

Rube"s face changed as she talked. His jaw clenched tight. His hands,

those huge hands that had been so gentle throwing a baseball, curled

into fists. His whole body tensed like a coiled spring.

"Where is he?" Rube"s voice was low and dangerous. "Where"s this

guy now?"

"Still at the house. Painting."

Rube took a step toward the house, then stopped. McGinty saw him

fighting with himself, saw the rage warring with something else. Reason,

maybe. Or fear.

"Little Miss," he said, and his voice was shaking now. "I can"t do nothing. You understand? I got a record. I get into trouble with the cops, they"ll put me away. I won"t be able to work. Won"t be able to

help my boy."

His fists were still clenched, knuckles white. "I want to. God knows I

want to go over there and teach that guy what it feels like to be hit by

someone bigger than him. But I can"t. I just can"t."

Tears were running down Rube"s face now, mixing with the anger on his

features. McGinty had never seen a grown man cry before. Not like this.

Not with rage and frustration and helplessness all mixed together.

"Little Miss, you need to tell your mom. Right now. She"ll know what

to do. And maybe'..." He looked toward The Derby. "Maybe you tell

Lefty too. He don"t have the same problems I do."

McGinty nodded and ran toward her house. Behind her, she heard Rube

punching something. Probably the brick wall. Probably hurting himself.

But she didn"t look back.

'* '* '*

Her mother was hanging laundry in the back yard. When she saw McGinty"s

face, she dropped the wet sheet she was holding.

"What"s wrong? What happened?"

McGinty told her everything. About the painter and the baby and the

hitting and the words. Her mother"s face went from concerned to furious.

"That son of a'..." She caught herself, took a deep breath. "Okay. Okay. We"re going to handle this. First, we"re going over there right

now and getting that man away from that baby. Then we"re calling Mrs.

Kowalski. And then'..."

She looked toward The Derby, her jaw set. "Then I"m going to have a

word with Lefty."

They walked quickly to the Kowalskis" house. The painter was back

outside now, working on the trim around the windows like nothing had

happened. He saw them coming and smiled, that same respectable smile.

"Afternoon, ma"am."

McGinty"s mother didn"t smile back. "My daughter says she saw you hit

Mrs. Kowalski"s baby. That true?"

The painter"s smile didn"t falter. "Baby was crying, making it hard to work. I just patted him a little to quiet him down. That"s all. Your

daughter must have misunderstood what she saw."

"My daughter doesn"t misunderstand. And she doesn"t lie."

"Well, maybe she needs glasses then. Because I didn"t do nothing wrong. Just trying to do my job here."

Inside the house, the baby started crying again. The painter"s jaw tightened, his mask slipping just a little. McGinty saw the anger in his

eyes, the same anger she"d seen through the window.

"You"re done here," McGinty"s mother said firmly. "Pack up your things and leave. Now."

"You can"t tell me to leave. This ain"t your house."

"No, but I can tell Mrs. Kowalski what you did. And I can tell every other woman on this street. You"ll never work in this neighborhood

again."

The painter"s eyes narrowed. "Your daughter"s a liar. And you"re a—-"

"Careful." The voice came from behind them. Lefty. He"d appeared like

a ghost, silent and sudden. Two of his men flanked him. "Very careful

what you say next."

The painter looked at Lefty, and McGinty saw recognition flash across

his face. Everyone in the neighborhood knew Lefty.

"This ain"t your business," the painter said, but his voice had lost its confidence.

"Everything in this neighborhood is my business. Especially when it

involves hitting babies and threatening little girls." Lefty"s voice was calm, conversational even. But there was steel underneath it. "Now,

I"m going to make this simple for you. You"re going to pack up your

brushes and your paint and your ladder. You"re going to leave. And you"re not coming back. Not to this house. Not to this street. Not to

this neighborhood."

"Or what?"

Lefty smiled, but it wasn"t a friendly smile. "Or my friends here will help you pack. And trust me, you don"t want their help. It tends to be'... rough."

The two men with Lefty took a step forward. Big men. The kind who knew

how to handle themselves.

The painter looked at them, then at Lefty, then back at McGinty"s mother. Whatever he saw in their faces made him decide. He started

gathering his things, throwing brushes into a bucket, closing paint cans

with angry movements.

"This ain"t right," he muttered. "I didn"t do nothing wrong. Kid probably deserved it anyway, crying all the time."

Lefty"s hand shot out faster than McGinty could follow. He grabbed the

painter by his shirt collar and pulled him close.

"Listen to me very carefully," Lefty said quietly. "You ever lay hands on a kid again, I"ll hear about it. And if I hear about it, I"ll find you. And when I find you, I"ll make sure you can"t hurt anyone

ever again. We clear?"

The painter nodded, his face pale.

"Good. Now get out of here. And remember, I got friends in every neighborhood in this city. You can"t hide from me."

Lefty released him, and the painter stumbled back. He finished packing

in silence, loaded everything into an old truck, and drove away
without
looking back.

'* '* '*

After he was gone, McGinty"s mother thanked Lefty. "I appreciate
what
you did. That man'..."
"Was a piece of garbage," Lefty finished. "Worse than any of the
guys
sleeping in the alley. At least they"re honest about what they are."
He looked down at McGinty. "You did good, kid. Telling someone.
That
took guts."
"I told Rube first. But he said he couldn"t do anything."
Lefty nodded. "Rube"s smart. He knows his limitations. Man"s got
a
record, can"t be getting into fights. But he did the right thing
sending you to get help." He straightened his jacket. "I"m going to
go talk to him. Make sure he"s okay."
McGinty and her mother went inside. A little later, Mrs. Kowalski
came
home and they told her everything. She cried and held her baby
and
thanked them over and over.
That night, McGinty couldn"t sleep. She kept seeing the painter"s
face. How normal he looked. How respectable. How wrong she"d
been about
him.
She thought about the people everyone said were bad. Mossy, with
his
rotting legs and his terrible smell. The Butcher, with his fake

disability and his panhandling. Jimmy, always shaking and drunk. Rube, a

big scary man with a criminal record.

But when had any of them hurt a baby? When had any of them threatened a

child? When had any of them pretended to be something they weren"t?

They were honest about what they were. They didn"t hide behind clean

clothes and slicked-back hair. They didn"t pretend to be respectable while doing terrible things in private.

"* "* "*

The next day, McGinty found Rube in the alley. His knuckles were bruised

and swollen. He"d definitely punched something hard.

"Rube, your hands'..."

He looked down at them and shrugged. "Needed to hit something. Better a

wall than a person I"d go to jail for."

"I"m sorry you couldn"t help."

Rube crouched down to her level. "But I did help, Little Miss. I helped

by knowing my limits. I helped by sending you to people who could do

something. That"s the smart play."

"But you wanted to do more."

"Of course I did. I wanted to tear that guy apart. But wanting to do something and being able to do it, those are two different things. A man"s got to know the difference."

He stood up, flexing his bruised knuckles. "Your dad taught me that.

He"d get so mad sometimes, at the unfairness of things. At how hard

life was. But he"d hold it in. Control it. Because losing control meant

losing everything else. His job. His family. His dignity."

"Did he ever hit walls?"

Rube smiled sadly. "Oh yeah. Plenty of times. Sometimes that"s all you

can do. Hit a wall and walk away."

McGinty thought about that. About her father hitting walls instead of

people. About Rube knowing his limits. About doing what you could, not

what you wanted to do.

"Rube? People think you"re bad because you"ve been in trouble. But

that painter, everyone thought he was good. Because he had a job and

clean clothes."

"Yeah."

"But they were wrong. About both of you."

Rube looked at her for a long moment. "You"re a smart kid, Little

Miss. Smarter than most adults. Yeah, people get it wrong all the time.

They judge by what they see on the outside. But what matters is what"s

inside. What you do when nobody"s looking. How you treat people who

can"t fight back."

He pulled out his baseball from his pocket, the one they used for catch.

"By that measure, I"m no saint. I"ve done bad things. Got a record to

prove it. But I never hurt a kid. Never would. And that painter? He can

wear all the nice clothes he wants. Inside, he"s rotten."

McGinty nodded. She understood now. Really understood.

"* "* "*

That night, McGinty lay in bed thinking about justice. The painter had

hurt a baby and got away with it. Sort of. He didn"t go to jail. The
police were never called.

But he"d been run out of the neighborhood. He"d been threatened by

Lefty. He"d been scared. And according to what she"d overheard from

her mother, word had spread. The painter wouldn"t find work anywhere in

the area. Maybe not anywhere in the city, if Lefty"s reach was as long

as he said.

Was that justice? The nuns at school would say no. They"d say justice

came from the law, from courts and judges and policemen.

But McGinty had seen how the law worked. Or didn"t work. She"d seen

the police ignore Mossy and The Butcher, let them sleep in doorways

because it was easier than dealing with them. She"d seen them hassle

Rube for no reason except he was big and had a record.

The law protected respectable people like the painter. It didn"t
protect babies. It didn"t protect the Bottle Babies. It didn"t protect

people like her father, who worked hard but couldn"t quite keep it together.

But Lefty"s justice? That worked. It was fast and sure and it protected

the people who needed protecting.

McGinty knew what the nuns would say about that. They"d say it was

wrong. They"d say you can"t take the law into your own hands. They"d

say bad men doing good things were still bad men.

But lying there in the dark, McGinty couldn"t make herself believe it.

Because when it mattered, when a baby needed protecting and a child

needed help, it wasn"t the police or the priests or the respectable people who showed up.

It was Lefty. It was Rube, knowing his limits but still caring. It was her mother, standing up to someone even though she was scared.

It was the people who lived in the gray spaces, who couldn"t be sorted

neatly into good and bad. The people who did whatever needed doing,

whether it was legal or not, whether it was proper or not.

The people who looked after their own.

And maybe that was the most important kind of justice. The kind that

actually worked. The kind that actually protected people.

McGinty thought about her father. About how he"d lived in that gray

space too. Working for bookies. Drinking too much. But also protecting his family. Being kind to men who had nothing. Vouching for Jimmy so he

could get work.

Not a perfect man. Not a respectable man. But a good man, in the ways

that mattered.

And she was his daughter. She"d carry that forward. That understanding

that the world wasn"t simple. That good and bad weren"t always clear.

That sometimes you had to look past the surface to see what someone

really was.

Outside, the alley was quiet. Somewhere in his cardboard fortress, Mossy

slept. Somewhere else, The Butcher and Jimmy rested in whatever shelter

they"d found. Rube was probably home with his wife and son.

And the painter was gone. Run out of the neighborhood by a bookie with a

code of honor.

The world, McGinty thought, was a very complicated place. But at least

she was starting to understand it.

Chapter 10: Spring and Small Miracles

Spring finally arrived for real in late March. Not the false starts
they"d had before, but actual spring with warm sun and birds
singing
and green things pushing up through the dirt.

McGinty woke up one Saturday morning to sunlight streaming
through her
window. Not the weak winter sun, but bright golden light that
made
everything look new. She dressed quickly and ran downstairs.

"Ma, can I go outside?"

Her mother looked up from her coffee. There were still dark circles
under her eyes from working double shifts, but she was smiling.
"Go on.

Just don"t go too far."

McGinty burst into the back yard. The patchy grass was trying to
turn
green. The scraggly tree by the fence had tiny buds on its branches.
Even the alley looked better, the cinders washed clean by spring
rains.

And there, in the alley, she saw Rube. But he wasn"t alone.

A boy was with him, maybe eight or nine years old, with dark hair
and
Rube"s same wide smile. He was throwing a baseball to his father,
and
Rube was catching it with his bare hands, no mitt needed.

"That"s it, Tommy!" Rube called out. "Nice throw! Put your whole
body into it!"

The boy threw again, harder this time. Rube caught it easily and
tossed
it back. They were both laughing.

McGinty watched from the gate, not wanting to interrupt. This was

something special. Something private.

But Rube saw her and waved her over. "Little Miss! Come here, I want

you to meet someone. Tommy, this is my friend McGinty. McGinty, this is

my son Tommy."

The boy looked at her shyly. "Hi."

"Hi."

"You want to play catch with us?" Rube asked. "I got an extra mitt."

McGinty nodded eagerly. Rube produced her old mitt, the one they"d used

before, and they formed a triangle in the alley. Tommy threw to McGinty,

McGinty threw to Rube, Rube threw to Tommy. Around and around, the ball

flying through the spring air.

Tommy was good. Much better than McGinty. He could catch high throws and

low throws and even throws that went a little wild. And when he threw,

the ball went exactly where he wanted it to go.

"You"re really good," McGinty told him after a particularly impressive catch.

Tommy blushed. "My dad taught me. He says I might be able to play for

the school team next year."

"You will," Rube said, his voice full of pride. "You"re better than I was at your age. Way better."

They played for almost an hour. McGinty watched Rube with his son and

felt something twist in her chest. This was what a father should be. Teaching his kid. Being proud of him. Spending time with him.

Her own father had done these things too. Before the drinking got bad.

Before the accident. She remembered him teaching her to tie her shoes,

to ride a bike with training wheels, to count to one hundred.

"You okay, Little Miss?" Rube had stopped playing and was looking at

her with concern.

McGinty wiped her eyes quickly. "Yeah. Just'... I miss my dad. That"s

all."

Rube nodded slowly. He looked at Tommy, then back at McGinty. "Tommy,

why don"t you practice throwing at that mark on the wall over there? I

need to talk to McGinty for a minute."

Tommy ran off, happy to show off his accuracy. Rube sat down on a crate

and gestured for McGinty to sit beside him.

"Your dad loved you very much, you know that? He talked about you all

the time. About how smart you were, how strong you were."

"Then why"d he drink so much? Why"d he leave us?"

Rube was quiet for a moment. "He didn"t mean to leave you. The drinking, it"s like'... it"s like a monster that gets inside you. Your dad fought it as hard as he could. Some days he won. Some days the monster won."

"Are you fighting a monster too?"

"Every day. But I got something your dad didn"t have as much of. I got

fear. I"m so scared of losing Tommy, of not being there for him, that it keeps me from drinking as much. The fear is stronger than the thirst,

most days."

"But you still drink sometimes."

"Yeah. I do. And I"m not proud of it. But I"m trying, Little Miss. That"s all any of us can do. Keep trying." He looked at his son, throwing the ball with perfect form. "Your dad tried too. Right up until the end, he was trying. Don"t ever forget that."

'* '* '*

The next week brought another small miracle. McGinty was walking past

The Derby when she saw Jimmy sweeping the front steps. Nothing unusual

about that. But something was different.

His hands weren"t shaking.

McGinty stopped and stared. Jimmy"s hands were moving steady and sure,

the broom handle held firm. His face looked different too. Less gray.

Less haunted.

"Jimmy?"

He looked up and smiled. A real smile that reached his eyes. "Morning,

Little Miss. Beautiful day, isn"t it?"

"Your hands'..."

Jimmy held them out, looking at them like they belonged to someone else.

"Three weeks. Haven"t had a drink in three weeks. The shaking stopped about five days ago."

"That"s'... that"s really good, Jimmy."

"It is. Lefty"s been helping me. Gave me more hours, more responsibility. Says if I can make it to a month, he"ll put me on regular payroll. With benefits." Jimmy"s voice wavered a little. "Haven"t been on regular payroll in six years."

Lefty appeared in the doorway. "Jimmy"s doing good work. Real good.

Proud of him."

Jimmy ducked his head, embarrassed by the praise but clearly pleased.

"Thank you, boss."

"Keep it up," Lefty said, then disappeared back inside.

Jimmy went back to sweeping, and McGinty watched his steady hands. Three

weeks. Maybe it wouldn"t last. Maybe tomorrow he"d be shaking again.

But today, right now, Jimmy was sober. He was working. He had hope.

Small miracles.

'* '* '*

The third miracle came from an unexpected source. McGinty was in the

alley one afternoon when she noticed The Butcher wasn"t in his usual

spot near the loading dock. She asked Mossy if he"d seen him.

Mossy grunted and pointed toward the bicycle shop. "Got himself a room.

In the basement. Owner"s letting him stay there in exchange for watching the place at night."

"A room? Like, inside?"

"Yeah. Got a cot and everything. Even got heat." Mossy spat to the side. "Lucky bastard."

Later, McGinty saw The Butcher coming out of the bicycle shop. He looked

different. Cleaner. His clothes were still old and patched, but they"d

been washed recently. His hair was combed. And he was walking straighter, with more confidence.

"Hey, kid," he called out when he saw her. "Hear about my new digs?"

"Mossy told me. That"s really good."

"Yeah. It ain"t much. Just a small room in the basement. But it"s got

walls. And a door that locks. And I don"t have to worry about rain or

snow or punks trying to steal my stuff." He pulled out some coins from

his pocket. "Here. For you. I know you like the movies."

McGinty took the coins. Two quarters. Enough for a movie and popcorn.

"Thank you."

"You"re a good kid. Always been nice to me, even when others weren"t.

I don"t forget that." The Butcher adjusted his crutch. "Your old man

was the same way. Always treated me like I was a person, not just some

bum."

He hobbled off, and McGinty watched him go. The Butcher had a room. A

real room with walls and a door. It wasn"t much by most people"s standards. But for him, it was everything.

"* "* "*

Even Mossy seemed different. Not better, exactly. His legs were still a

mess, his smell was still overwhelming, and he still spent most of his

time drunk. But he seemed less angry. Less mean.

One afternoon, McGinty saw him actually sharing his Sneaky Pete with

another Bottle Baby who"d wandered into the area. Sharing. Mossy. The

man who never shared anything.

She mentioned it to Rube when she saw him later. Rube laughed. "Spring

does that sometimes. Makes people feel a little more hopeful. A little

more generous. Won"t last forever. Come winter, Mossy"ll be his old

mean self again. But for now? Let him enjoy it."

"* "* "*

One Saturday in April, exactly one year after her father died, McGinty

asked her mother if she could plant flowers by the back gate.

"Flowers? Where"d you get money for flowers?"

"The Butcher gave me some. I saved it up."

Her mother"s face softened. "For your father?"

McGinty nodded. "I want something pretty to remember him by. Something

that grows."

They went to the garden store together and bought a flat of marigolds.

Bright orange and yellow, tough flowers that could survive city

conditions. Back home, McGinty dug a small patch of dirt near the gate and planted them carefully, just like the man at the store had shown her.

When she was done, she sat back and looked at them. Small and fragile

now, but they"d grow. They"d bloom. They"d last the whole summer.

"Hi, Daddy," she whispered. "I planted these for you. So you"ll always be here with us."

Her mother put a hand on her shoulder and squeezed gently. They stood

there together for a long moment, looking at the flowers.

'* '* '*

The next day, McGinty came out to water the flowers and stopped short.

Someone had put rocks around the flower bed. Nice rocks, smooth and

rounded, creating a little border to protect the plants.

She looked up and saw Rube watching from down the alley. He waved.

"Thought they could use some protection. Don"t want nobody stepping on

them by accident."

"Thank you, Rube."

"Your dad would have liked this. He always said this neighborhood needed more flowers. More pretty things to look at."

Over the next few days, other things appeared. Someone left a small packet of fertilizer. Someone else left an old coffee can full of water in case McGinty needed it for watering. Even The Butcher contributed,

leaving a stick that could be used as a stake if the flowers grew tall.

The most surprising contribution came from Mossy. McGinty was watering the flowers one evening when she noticed a small hand-lettered sign

stuck in the ground: "Don"t Touch." The handwriting was shaky and

barely legible, but the message was clear.

Mossy was protecting the flowers.

McGinty walked down to his spot. He was lying in his usual place, a tin

cup of Sneaky Pete in his hand. When he saw her coming, he grunted.

"Thank you for the sign," McGinty said.

Mossy waved his hand dismissively. "Flowers are nice. Ain"t enough

nice things around here. Somebody"s gotta make sure they survive."

He looked at her with his rheumy eyes. "Your old man, he was always

talking about planting a garden. Said he wanted to grow tomatoes. Never

got around to it. These flowers, they"re good. He"d like them."

"I hope so."

"I know so. Now get out of here. I got drinking to do."

But Mossy was smiling. Just a little. Just enough.

'* '* '*

As spring deepened into early summer, the flowers grew. They bloomed

bright and cheerful, adding color to the gray alley. McGinty watered

them every day, and the Bottle Babies watched over them like guardians.

Jimmy stopped to look at them on his way to work at The Derby.

"Beautiful," he"d say. "Just beautiful."

The Butcher would adjust the rocks around them if any got moved. "Gotta

keep things neat," he"d explain. "Show some respect."

Rube brought Tommy by to see them. "See, son? This is what McGinty

planted for her dad. To remember him by. That"s what love looks like.

Taking care of something, even after someone"s gone."

And Mossy? Mossy kept his sign there and chased away anyone who got too

close. "Stay back! Them flowers ain"t for touching!"

One warm evening in May, McGinty sat by the flowers and thought about

her father. About all the things he"d taught her, even if he didn"t

know he was teaching them. About seeing people for who they really were.

About kindness in unexpected places. About how life was complicated and

people were complicated and that was okay.

The flowers waved gently in the breeze, bright and alive. Just like the

memories of her father. Just like the hope that spring brought.

Small miracles. That"s what this spring had brought. Jimmy"s steady

hands. The Butcher"s room. Mossy"s generosity. Rube"s pride in his

son. And these flowers, protected by a neighborhood of broken men who

understood the importance of keeping something beautiful alive.

McGinty smiled and touched one of the marigold petals. Soft and strong

at the same time.

"Thanks, Daddy," she whispered. "For teaching me to see."

And in the warm spring air, surrounded by the sounds of the neighborhood
she loved, McGinty felt her father"s presence. Not sad anymore. Not
haunted by what he"d been at the end. But grateful for what he"d given
her.
The ability to see past surfaces. To find dignity in unlikely places. To
understand that everyone was fighting their own battles, carrying their
own monsters.
And most importantly, to know that people deserved respect. All people.
No matter where they slept or how they lived or what battles they were
losing.
Everyone deserved to be seen. Really seen.
The marigolds bloomed on, bright promises in a gray world. And the
Bottle Babies kept watch, protecting these small miracles just as
fiercely as they"d been protected themselves.

Chapter 11: The Fish Store Check Delivery

The first Thursday of every month, like clockwork, Rube would disappear

into the fish store for about fifteen minutes. McGinty had noticed this

pattern but never thought much about it until one day in June when she

happened to be nearby and saw him emerge with two envelopes in his

massive hands.

He walked down the alley with purpose, holding the envelopes carefully

like they were precious things. Which, McGinty realized, they were.

She followed at a distance, curious.

Rube went to Mossy"s spot first. Mossy was in his usual place,

half-asleep in his cardboard fortress. Rube crouched down and knocked

gently on the tar paper that served as Mossy"s door.

"Mossy. It"s Rube. Got your check."

Mossy emerged, blinking in the daylight. For once, he wasn"t growling

or spitting. He reached out with trembling hands and took the envelope.

"Thanks, Rube."

"You want me to take you to the bank? Help you cash it?"

Mossy shook his head. "Fish store"ll do it. Already talked to them."

"Okay. You let me know if you need anything."

Rube moved on to The Butcher"s spot near the bicycle shop. The Butcher
was sitting on his cot in the basement room, reading an old newspaper.

When he saw Rube with the envelope, his face lit up.

"That time already?"

"First Thursday. Like always." Rube handed over the envelope. "Got
your name on it and everything."

The Butcher opened it right there and pulled out the check. He stared at
it for a long moment. "Never thought I"d be grateful for losing this leg in Korea. But this check'... it"s the difference between eating and not eating. Between having a place to sleep and freezing to death."

"I know. Same for Mossy. His check keeps him going."

"You"re a good man, Rube. Coming every month like this. Never missing.
Never taking a cut even though you could."

"It"s not my money. Never would be." Rube stood up. "You take care
now."

After Rube left, McGinty waited a minute, then approached The Butcher"s
door. He saw her and waved her in.

"Come to see my fancy accommodations?" He gestured around the small
basement room. It was clean but sparse. A cot. A chair. A small hot plate. An old trunk that held his belongings. But it had concrete walls
that didn"t leak and a small window that let in light.

"It"s nice," McGinty said honestly.

"It"s a palace compared to sleeping under cardboard." The Butcher sat

down on his cot. "You want to know about the checks, don"t you? I saw

you following Rube."

McGinty nodded.

"Me and Mossy, we both served. I was in Korea, he was in the First World War. When you serve and you get injured or sick, the government"s

supposed to take care of you. They send checks every month. Disability,

they call it."

"But you don"t have houses. How do they send the checks?"

"That"s where the fish store comes in. The owner, Mr. Kaplan, he lets

us use the store as our mailing address. The checks come there, and Rube

picks them up and brings them to us. Then we go to the fish store or the

bank, and we cash them."

"Why does Mr. Kaplan do that?"

The Butcher smiled. "Because he"s a decent man. And because he knows

what it"s like to serve. His brother died in World War Two. He figures

if his brother had made it home hurt like us, he"d want someone to help

him. So he helps us."

"* "* "*

That afternoon, McGinty went to the fish store. She"d been inside a few times with her mother, but she"d never really paid attention. Now she

looked at it with new eyes.

The store was long and narrow, with fish displayed on crushed ice in

cases along one side. The smell was overwhelming. Sharp and salty and

fishy all at once. Men in white aprons and rubber boots worked behind

the counter, cutting and cleaning and wrapping.

Mr. Kaplan stood at the register, an older man with gray hair and a kind

face lined by years of hard work. He saw McGinty and smiled.

"Hello, young lady. Need something for your mother?"

"No, sir. I wanted to ask you something."

"Ask away."

"Why do you help the Bottle Babies? With their checks and everything?"

Mr. Kaplan was quiet for a moment. Then he gestured for her to follow

him to a quiet corner of the store.

"You know what it means to serve your country?"

"Like in the war?"

"Yes. When you serve, you"re saying you"ll put your life on the line for everyone else. For people you don"t even know. Mossy did that. So

did The Butcher. So did a lot of men who didn"t make it home, including

my brother David."

His eyes got distant. "David was killed in France in 1944. Twenty-three years old. Had his whole life ahead of him. And he died so people like

me could live free."

"I"m sorry."

"Me too. Every day. But you know what would make me even more sorry? If

I saw men who served like David did and I turned my back on them just

because they"re down on their luck. Just because they drink or smell

bad or sleep in doorways." He looked at her seriously. "They earned my

respect. They earned everyone"s respect. And if all I can do is let them use my address for their checks, that"s what I"ll do."

"Did my father get checks here too?"

Mr. Kaplan nodded. "For a while, yes. After his accident, he couldn"t

work as steady. He had some benefits coming from his service, not much,

but something. I held them for him and let him cash them here. No charge

for cashing. That was between him and me."

McGinty felt tears prick at her eyes. Her father had been here, in this

store, cashing checks just like Mossy and The Butcher. Her father had

needed help just like they did.

"Your father was a good man," Mr. Kaplan said gently. "Proud man. It

killed him to have to ask for help. But he did it for you and your mother and your sisters. That takes courage."

"* "* "*

Later that day, McGinty found Rube stacking crates behind the fish store. His shift wasn"t over yet, but he took a break when he saw her.

"Little Miss. What"s on your mind?"

"I saw you delivering the checks today. To Mossy and The Butcher."

Rube nodded. "Been doing it for two years now. Ever since Mr. Kaplan
asked me to."

"Why you?"

"Because he trusts me. And because the other Bottle Babies trust me. If
someone they didn"t know came around with their checks, they might
think it was a trick. They might not take them. But they know me. They
know I"m not going to steal from them or cheat them."

Rube sat down on a crate, and McGinty sat beside him. "It"s important
work, Little Miss. Those checks, they"re the only money Mossy and The
Butcher have. Without them, they"d starve. Or worse."

"Do you get paid for delivering them?"

"No. And I wouldn"t take money if Mr. Kaplan offered it. This is something I do because it"s right. Because these men served their country and they deserve to get what"s owed to them."

He looked down at his big hands. "I got a record, like I told you. Done
some things I"m not proud of. But this? This is something good. Something I can feel proud of. Mr. Kaplan trusts me with his time and
his respect. That means something to a man like me."

"My dad had the same thing," McGinty said quietly. "With the parking

lot job. It made him feel proud."

"Your dad understood. A man needs something to be proud of. Something

that makes him feel like he matters. For me, it"s delivering these

checks and taking care of my son. For your dad, it was that parking lot

job and taking care of his family."

Rube stood up and went back to stacking crates. McGinty watched him

work. There was dignity in it. In the careful way he moved the crates.

In the way he made sure they were stable and secure. In the pride he

took in doing his job well.

* * *

That evening, McGinty told her mother about what she"d learned. About

the checks and Mr. Kaplan and Rube"s deliveries. Her mother listened,

nodding.

"Mr. Kaplan is one of the good ones," her mother said. "There are

people in this world who help quietly. They don"t make a big show of

it. They don"t expect thanks or recognition. They just see someone who

needs help and they help. That"s real charity."

"Not like the church ladies who come around with their baskets and

their pity faces?"

Her mother smiled ruefully. "Exactly. Those women, they want you to feel grateful and small. They want you to know they"re better than you,

that they"re doing you a favor. But Mr. Kaplan? He helps because it"s

the right thing to do. He helps with respect."

She sat down at the kitchen table, her face tired but thoughtful. "When

your father was at his worst, when he could barely work anymore, a lot

of people turned their backs on us. Family. Friends. People from church.

But you know who helped? Mr. Kaplan. Lefty. The fish store workers. The

men your father worked with. The ones people said were no good."

"Why do you think that is, Ma?"

"Because they understood. They"d been down. They"d needed help. They

knew what it was like to be looked down on, to be judged. So when they

saw someone else struggling, they didn"t turn away. They helped."

Her mother reached across the table and took McGinty"s hand. "You"re

learning important things, sweetheart. You"re learning that help comes

from unexpected places. That goodness isn"t always where you think

it"ll be. And that the people everyone else looks down on, they"re often the ones with the biggest hearts."

"* "* "*

The next first Thursday, McGinty watched from a distance as Rube went to the fish store and emerged with the two envelopes. She followed him

again as he made his rounds, this time not hiding.

When he finished delivering the checks, he turned and saw her. He smiled

and waved her over.

"You watching my route now?"

"I just wanted to see. To understand."

"And do you understand?"

McGinty thought about it. About Mr. Kaplan and his dead brother. About

Rube"s pride in being trusted. About Mossy and The Butcher depending on

those checks. About the quiet web of support that kept everyone going.

"I think I do. It"s not about money. It"s about respect. About making

sure people get what they earned. About being reliable so people can

count on you."

Rube"s face broke into a wide smile. "That"s exactly right, Little Miss. You got it. You really got it."

He pulled out his baseball from his pocket. "Come on. We got time for a

quick catch before I have to get back to work."

They played catch in the alley, the ball flying back and forth between

them. McGinty thought about her father, about how he must have felt with

his parking lot job. The pride. The purpose. The feeling of being needed

and trusted.

And she thought about all the people in the neighborhood who helped each
other in small ways. Mr. Kaplan with his mailing address. Lefty with his
jobs and protection. Her mother with her sandwiches for Jimmy. Rube with
his check deliveries and his kindness to a grieving girl.

The Chinese restaurant workers with their extra fortune cookies. The
bicycle shop owner with his basement room. Even Mossy with his grudging
protection of the flowers.

It was a network. A safety net made of small kindnesses and quiet help.

Not dramatic or glamorous. Not the kind of thing that made headlines or
won awards.

Just people looking out for each other. Taking care of their own. Making
sure nobody fell through the cracks.

And that, McGinty realized as she caught another throw from Rube, was
what community really meant. Not the fancy definition from school. Not
the neat picture of neighbors waving to each other on perfect streets.

But this. This messy, complicated, imperfect network of people helping
each other survive. People who had nothing giving what little they had.

People who"d been knocked down helping others get back up.

"You"re getting good at this," Rube called out as she caught a high throw. "Real good. Your dad would be proud."

McGinty smiled and threw the ball back. Her father would be proud. Not

just of her catching skills, but of everything else she was learning.

How to see people. How to understand the complicated ways people helped

each other. How to recognize dignity in unexpected places.

And most importantly, how to be part of that network herself. To look

out for others. To help in whatever small ways she could.

The ball flew back and forth in the summer air, a simple game connecting

them across generations and circumstances. And in that moment, McGinty

felt it all come together. The lessons. The understanding. The wisdom

her father had given her without even knowing it.

Everyone mattered. Everyone deserved respect. And everyone, no matter

how broken they seemed, had something to give.

Chapter 12: Lessons from the Broken

One year. Three hundred and sixty-five days since McGinty had stood in
the funeral home, her hand clutching her mother's coat, staring at the
closed casket that held her father. She hadn't understood then why it
had to be closed, but her mother had explained in that quiet, careful
way she had of delivering hard truths.

'The accident did too much damage, sweetheart. It's better this way.
Better to remember him as he was.'

But McGinty did remember him as he was. She remembered the
smell of
cheap whiskey on his breath when he tucked her in at night, his
hands
shaking as he tried to smooth her hair. She remembered how he'd
sing to
her sometimes, old songs from before the war, his voice cracking on
the
high notes. She remembered the way he'd looked at her mother, a
mixture
of love and shame that McGinty hadn't had words for then but
understood
now with a clarity that made her chest ache.

He'd been broken, her father. The war had cracked something
inside him,
and the garage accident had shattered what remained. The alcohol
was
just the glue he'd used to try to hold the pieces together, and it
hadn't worked. It never worked.

McGinty stood at the back gate now, in almost the exact spot where she'd

stood that day one year ago when everything had felt raw and impossible.

The alley looked the same—-the same cinders, the same loading docks,

the same cardboard fortresses. But McGinty wasn't the same. She'd turned

eight last month, and though that was only one year older, it felt like

a lifetime.

The morning air carried the first real warmth of spring. Crocuses had

pushed up through the dirt near the fence, purple and white blooms that

seemed impossibly delicate against the industrial grey of the alley.

McGinty had planted them last fall, bulbs she'd bought with money she'd

saved from returning bottles. She'd planted them for her father, though

she'd never told anyone that.

A sound drew her attention—-voices, low and urgent, coming from Mossy's

corner. McGinty moved closer, her feet finding the familiar path through

the cinders without conscious thought. She'd walked this route so many

times now that her body knew it by heart.

A new man sat on the concrete ledge near Mossy's cardboard fortress. He

was younger than the others, maybe thirty, with dark hair that fell across his forehead and clothes that, while dirty, weren't yet the terminal rags that marked the longtime residents of the alley. His hands

trembled as he held a tin cup, and his eyes had that hollow, hunted look

McGinty had seen before.

Rube stood nearby, his massive frame casting a shadow across the newcomer. The Butcher leaned against his crutch a few feet away, his

single eye fixed on the new man with an expression McGinty couldn't

quite read. Even Mossy had emerged from his cardboard den, his infected

legs wrapped in cleaner rags than usual, his fedora pushed back on his

head.

'Name's Walter,' the new man was saying, his voice rough with disuse.

'Got discharged from the Navy six months ago. Couldn't... couldn't make

it work.'

McGinty watched as Rube lowered himself to sit on a milk crate, bringing

himself closer to Walter's eye level. It was something McGinty had seen

him do before, this gentle giant making himself smaller so others wouldn't feel so small.

'Korea?' Rube asked.

Walter nodded, his eyes on the cup in his hands. 'Inchon. I was on a

ship when...' He trailed off, and nobody pushed him to finish.

'Listen,' Rube said, his voice carrying that particular gentleness he used when he was being careful with words. 'This place, it ain't much.

But there's rules. You follow the rules, you'll be okay.'

The Butcher shifted his weight, his wooden leg scraping against the concrete. 'First rule,' he said, and his voice had an edge to it but not the meanness McGinty might have expected. 'Stay away from Mossy's spot

unless he says otherwise. He's particular about his space.'

Mossy grunted something that might have been agreement, his hand moving

to adjust the rags on his legs.

'Second rule,' Rube continued. 'The fish store owner, Mr. Goldstein,

he's good people. Don't do nothing to cause him trouble. He lets some of

us use his address for checks, and if you got military benefits coming,

he'll help you with that.'

'Third rule,' The Butcher added. 'You see the little girl around

here—-' he gestured with his chin toward McGinty, who hadn't realized

she'd been spotted, '—-you watch your language and your manners. Her

family's been good to us. We don't bring trouble to their door.'

Walter's eyes found McGinty, and she saw something flicker across his

face. Shame, maybe, or recognition. She wondered if he had a daughter

somewhere, a little girl who might be wondering where her daddy had

gone.

'Hi,' McGinty said, her voice clear in the morning air. 'I'm McGinty.'

Walter nodded, his throat working. 'Ma'am,' he managed.

The formality of it—-this broken man calling an eight-year-old girl 'ma'am'—-made something twist in McGinty's chest. She thought of her father, remembered how he'd insisted on manners even when he could barely stand, how he'd taught her to say please and thank you, to hold doors for people, to treat everyone with respect.

'Just McGinty is fine,' she said.

Rube stood, his knees cracking audibly. 'There's work sometimes,' he told Walter. 'The fish store needs help on busy days. The Derby might need someone to sweep. It ain't steady, but it's something. And when winter comes—' he paused, his eyes distant, '—you'll want to have enough for cardboard and maybe a blanket. The cold here, it'll kill you if you let it.'

McGinty watched this exchange with a feeling she couldn't quite name. It was like watching a play she'd seen before, but this time she understood all the dialogue, all the subtext beneath the words. These men, these Bottle Babies that people crossed the street to avoid, were teaching a new arrival how to survive. They were creating a community out of nothing, building dignity from scraps of cardboard and tin cups.

Her father had been part of this world, she realized. Not the alley
exactly, but this ecosystem of broken men trying to hold each other
up.

The mafia men at The Derby who'd given him the parking lot job,
the fish
store owner who'd let him cash checks when he'd needed it, even
the
Bottle Babies themselves who'd shared cigarettes and conversation
when
her father had still been able to walk to the alley.

They'd all been trying to save each other, in their way. And when
saving
wasn't possible, they'd at least been there, bearing witness to each
other's struggles, refusing to let any man disappear completely into
his
pain.

'Hey, Little Miss.'

McGinty turned to find Rube walking toward her, his massive
hand already
reaching for the baseball mitt tucked into his waistband. He'd
started
carrying it with him, she'd noticed, ever since that first game of
catch. Like he wanted to be ready in case she asked.

'You got time for a catch?' he asked.

McGinty nodded, feeling a smile tug at her lips. 'Yeah. Let me get
my
mitt.'

She ran to the house, her feet light on the cinders, and retrieved her
first baseman's mitt from where it hung on a nail by the back door.
Her
mother was in the kitchen, preparing lunch, and she looked up as
McGinty

burst through.

'Playing with Rube?' her mother asked.

'Yeah.'

Her mother's expression softened, and she set down her paring knife.

'Your father would have liked that,' she said quietly. 'He always said Rube was a good man. Said he just had bad luck.'

McGinty paused in the doorway, her mitt clutched to her chest. 'Daddy had bad luck too,' she said.

Her mother's eyes glistened, but she didn't look away. 'Yes,' she said. 'Yes, he did. But he had us, too. And that was good luck, wasn't it? The best luck.'

McGinty nodded, her throat tight. She thought about all the things her father had taught her, not through words but through how he'd lived. How he'd treated the Bottle Babies with respect when others scorned them.

How he'd tipped his hat to working girls on the Avenue when other men sneered. How he'd shared his cigarettes even when he couldn't afford them. How he'd loved them—-her mother, her sisters, her—-with a fierceness that alcohol couldn't quite drown.

'I miss him,' McGinty whispered.

'Me too, baby. Me too.' Her mother's voice was steady, strong. She'd learned how to be strong this year, McGinty realized. Or maybe she'd always been strong and McGinty was only now seeing it. 'But we're okay.

We're going to be okay.'

And McGinty believed her.

She ran back to the alley, where Rube waited with his mitt and a baseball. They found their usual spot, far enough from the cardboard fortresses to avoid interference but close enough to feel part of the alley's life.

Rube threw underhand, the way they'd established after that first accident. The ball sailed through the morning air, and McGinty caught it solidly in her mitt, the leather pocket cradling it perfectly. She threw it back, and they fell into the rhythm they'd developed over dozens of games—-throw, catch, throw, catch, the baseball a conversation between them that needed no words.

Walter watched from his spot near Mossy's corner. The Butcher had moved to sit beside him, sharing something from a flask. Even Mossy seemed interested, his massive head turned their direction.

After a while, McGinty called for a break and sat on an overturned milk crate. Rube settled himself on a stack of wooden pallets nearby, his breathing only slightly labored despite his size.

'Rube?' McGinty said.

'Yeah, Little Miss?'

'You're a good father.'

The words seemed to hit him physically. His shoulders tensed, and for a

moment McGinty worried she'd said something wrong. But then she saw his

eyes, and they were bright with unshed tears.

'I try,' he said, his voice rough. 'I don't get to see my boy as much as I'd like. His mother, she...' He trailed off, cleared his throat. 'But I

try. When I can work, I send money. And sometimes, when I've been good,

when I haven't been drinking too much, she lets me see him. Those are

good days.'

'My daddy tried too,' McGinty said. The words came out easier than she'd

expected. 'People said things about him. About the drinking and all. But

he tried. He loved us.'

Rube nodded slowly. 'I knew your daddy a little. We'd talk sometimes,

when he'd come through here. He was proud of you girls. Talked about you

all the time.'

McGinty felt something warm bloom in her chest. 'Really?'

'Really. He'd say, 'My McGinty, she's smart as a whip. Gonna do

something important someday." Rube smiled, and it transformed his rough

features into something gentle. 'Guess he was right about that. You already are doing something important.'

'What do you mean?'

'You see us, Little Miss. Really see us. Not what people say we are, not what we look like or smell like or where we sleep. You see who we are

underneath all that. That's rare. That's special.' He leaned forward, his elbows on his knees. 'You're wise beyond your years, you know that?

Eight years old and you already understand what most folks never figure

out.'

McGinty thought about this. She thought about Mossy, so frightening on

the surface but so careful never to threaten her. She thought about The

Butcher, who gave her nickels when he barely had two coins to rub together. She thought about Jimmy, who always knocked politely even

though the door was unlocked. She thought about Rube, who played catch

with her and called her 'Little Miss' and tried so hard to be a good father despite everything.

She thought about her father, who'd been both things at once—-a drunk

and a devoted father, a broken man and a loving husband, someone who'd

failed and someone who'd never stopped trying.

'My daddy taught me that,' she said finally. 'He didn't say it with words. But he showed me. He was nice to people. To you all. To everybody. He said everybody deserves respect.'

'He was right about that too.' Rube stood, brushing cinder dust from his

pants. 'Come on. Let's finish our game.'

They played for another twenty minutes, the baseball arcing back and forth between them in the spring sunshine. McGinty felt something settle

in her chest, some piece of the grief that had been sharp and jagged for

so long smoothing into something she could carry.

Her father was gone. That wouldn't change. But what he'd taught her,

what he'd shown her about kindness and dignity and seeing people for who

they really were—-that would stay. That would grow. She'd carry it forward like a torch passed hand to hand, lighting the way through whatever darkness came next.

As McGinty threw the ball one last time, she noticed Walter watching

them with an expression of longing so intense it made her chest ache. On

impulse, she called out to him.

'You want to play?'

Walter looked startled, his eyes darting to Rube as if seeking permission. Rube nodded encouragingly.

'I... I haven't thrown a ball in years,' Walter said.

'That's okay,' McGinty said. 'You can practice. That's what we're doing.

Practicing.'

Walter stood slowly, his hands trembling less than they had before. Rube

handed him the baseball, and Walter stared at it for a long moment, turning it over in his palms like it was something precious.

'Go ahead,' Rube said softly. 'She's tougher than she looks.'

Walter threw underhand, a gentle toss that McGinty caught easily. She threw it back, and Walter caught it with hands that remembered, even if

his mind had tried to forget.

They played until the lunch bells rang from the Catholic church three

blocks away. The Butcher had wandered closer, offering advice on Walter's form. Even Mossy watched from his cardboard throne, something

that might have been approval in his ravaged features.

As McGinty finally headed home, her mitt tucked under her arm and her

cheeks flushed from exertion, she felt lighter than she had in months.

The grief was still there—-it would always be there, she understood now. But it wasn't the only thing anymore. There was also this: the knowledge that kindness rippled outward, that dignity was something you

gave as much as received, that everyone was fighting battles you couldn't see.

At the gate, she turned back to look at the alley. The Bottle Babies were gathered now, Walter sitting among them like he'd always been

there. Rube caught her eye and raised his hand in a wave. McGinty waved

back.

Her father's flowers—-the crocuses she'd planted—-swayed gently in the

breeze, their purple blooms vivid against the grey. They'd come back,

she realized. Even after the winter, even after the cold that should have killed them, they'd come back.

Everything came back if you gave it a chance. Everything grew if you

tended it, even in the hardest soil.

McGinty went inside to where her mother was setting the table for lunch.

Her sisters were chattering about something that had happened at school,

their voices bright and quick. The kitchen smelled like tomato soup and

grilled cheese sandwiches.

Her mother looked up as McGinty entered, and something passed between

them—-an understanding, an acknowledgment. They were going to be okay.

It wouldn't be easy, and there would be hard days ahead. But they had

each other, and they had the lessons her father had left them, and that

was enough.

That was more than enough.

'Wash up for lunch, sweetheart,' her mother said.

McGinty went to the sink, pumping cold water over her hands and scrubbing away the cinder dust. Through the window above the sink, she

could see the alley, the sun casting long shadows across the cinders, the cardboard fortresses standing like small monuments to survival.

Everyone deserves respect, her father had taught her. Everyone has a

story. Everyone is fighting to survive.

And everyone—-even the broken, even the lost, even the ones society had

given up on—-everyone deserved compassion.

It was the most important lesson she'd ever learned, and she'd carry it

with her for the rest of her life.

McGinty dried her hands and went to join her family at the table, where

love and soup and ordinary conversation waited. Behind her, through the

window, the alley continued its daily rhythms—-men finding ways to

survive, to help each other, to maintain their dignity against all odds.

And in the dirt by the gate, purple crocuses bloomed.

THE END

Don't miss out!

Visit the website below and you can sign up to receive emails whenever P. A. Farrell publishes a new book. There's no charge and no obligation.

https://books2read.com/r/B-A-JNWAB-BSKZI

BOOKS 2 READ

Connecting independent readers to independent writers.

About the Author

P. A. Farrell is a psychologist and published author with McGraw-Hill, Springer Publishing, Cafe Lit, Ravens Perch, Humans of the World, Active Muse, Free Spirit Publishing, Scarlet Leaf Review, 100 Word Project, Woodcrest Magazine, Confetti, and LitBreak. She's a top health writer for Medium.com, has published self-help books, and is a board member of Clinics4Life. She lives on the East Coast of the US.

Read more at www.drfarrell.net.

www.ingramcontent.com/pod-product-compliance
Lightning Source LLC
Chambersburg PA
CBHW022130170626
46808CB00002B/934